MVA

D0917601

# #ABUSE OF DISCRETION

# Books by Pamela Samuels Young

### Vernetta Henderson Series

*Every Reasonable Doubt* (1st in series)

*In Firm Pursuit* (2nd in series)

*Murder on the Down Low* (3rd in series)

*Attorney-Client Privilege* (4th in series)

*Lawful Deception* (5th in series)

### Dre Thomas Series

*Buying Time* (1st in series)

*Anybody's Daughter* (2nd in series)

*Abuse of Discretion* (3rd in series)

### Young Adult Adaptations

*#Anybody's Daughter*

*#Abuse of Discretion*

### Short Stories

*The Setup*

*Easy Money*

*Unlawful Greed*

### Non-Fiction

*Kinky Coily: A Natural Hair Resource Guide*

# PAMELA SAMUELS YOUNG

# #ABUSE OF DISCRETION

#Abuse of Discretion

Goldman House Publishing

ISBN 978-0-9997331-1-0

For information about special discounts for bulk purchases, please contact the author or Goldman House Publishing.

Pamela Samuels Young
www.pamelasamuelsyoung.com

Goldman House Publishing
goldmanhousepublishing@gmail.com

**Printed in U.S.A.**

For my grand-nieces Anyah Samuels and Temple Samuels, and my grand-nephews, Blake Samuels and Roman Samuels, may you always be safe in this technologically complicated world.

"Why fit in when you're born to stand out?"

— Dr. Seuss

Trudging into her office, I sit down on a red cloth chair that's way more comfortable than the hard one outside. My heart is beating so fast it feels like it might jump out of my chest.

The only time I've ever been in Principal Keller's office was the day my dad enrolled me in school. Mrs. Singletary is standing in front of the principal's desk with her arms folded. I hope she's going to stay here with me, but a second later, she walks out and closes the door.

Principal Keller sits on the edge of her desk, looking down at me. "Graylin, do you have any inappropriate pictures on your cell phone?"

"Huh?" I try to keep a straight face. "No, ma'am."

"It's been brought to my attention that you have an inappropriate picture—a naked picture—of Kennedy Carlyle on your phone. Is that true?"

"No…uh…No, ma'am." *Thank God I deleted it!*

"This is a very serious matter, young man. So, I need you to tell me the truth."

"No, ma'am." I shake my head so hard my cheeks vibrate. "I don't have anything like that on my phone."

"I pray to God you're telling me the truth."

I don't want to ask this next question, but I have to know. "Um, so you called my dad?"

"Yes, I did. He's on his way down here now."

I hug myself and start rocking back and forth. Even though I deleted the picture, my dad is still going to kill me for having to leave work in the middle of the day.

"I also made another call."

At first I'm confused. Then I realize Mrs. Keller must've called my granny too. At least she'll keep my dad from going ballistic.

"So you called my granny?"

"No." The principal's cheeks puff up like she's about to blow something away. "I called the police."

*The police!*

My mouth is as dry as sand. "I don't have a naked picture of anybody on my phone, Mrs. Keller. I swear, I don't. Why'd you call the police on me?"

"I had no choice."

My right knee won't stop bouncing up and down. "Who said I had a naked picture?"

"I can't disclose that information."

There's a knock on the door. When two police officers step into the room, I almost pee on myself. They introduce themselves to the principal but ignore me.

One of the cops is short and Asian with biceps that look like two big rocks. He turns around and mean mugs me. "Is this the student?"

Principal Keller nods and hands him a piece of paper. He reads it, then turns back to me.

"I'm Officer Chin and this is Officer Fenton," the Asian cop says, referring to a tall white man with slicked-back hair. He's staring down at me too.

Officer Chin walks over and throws open the door to the principal's private conference room. "C'mon in here, young man. We need to have a little chat."

# CHAPTER 2

## Gus

I've been sitting in a chair outside the principal's office for more than twenty minutes now, getting more and more irritated. I don't know why, but something doesn't feel right.

*What the hell did Graylin do?*

I tried calling him, but got no answer. He must have his phone on mute since they aren't allowed to use it in class.

The door to the principal's office opens and Mrs. Keller shows me inside.

"What's going on? Where's Graylin?"

"Why don't you have a seat, Mr. Alexander?"

I sit down, but I'm still on edge. "I need to know what's going on with my son. Where is he?"

"I'm sorry to have to tell you this, but we received an anonymous report that Graylin had an inappropriate picture on his cell phone."

"What kind of inappropriate picture?"

"A photograph of a female classmate." Mrs. Keller swallows. "Naked."

I'm momentarily taken aback. My son's no angel, but this isn't something I would've expected from him. But then again, in this day and age with everything kids are exposed to and all this technology mess, who knows what they're up to. I start to breathe a little easier. A naked picture of a girl isn't the end of the world.

"Okay. I'll handle it. Who took the picture?"

"We don't know."

"Well, what did Graylin say about it?"

"He denied having it."

"Did you see the picture?"

"No."

"Then how do you know he has one?"

"As I said, we received an anonymous report."

"Did you check his phone?"

"No."

I'm not one of those parents who thinks my kid can do no wrong, but this sounds like something blown way out of proportion.

"So what you're telling me is that you don't even know if the allegation is true." And that's all it is as far as I'm concerned. An allegation and nothing more.

"You have to understand that when we receive a report like this, there's a certain protocol we have to follow."

I exhale. This is a bunch of crap. I can't believe I had to drive all the way down here for this bull.

"I'll talk to him. Where is he?"

"He's being interviewed by the police."

# CHAPTER 3

## *Graylin*

Once we're inside the principal's conference room, the white cop sits in the chair next to me and turns sideways, facing me. He's sitting so close that his knee keeps brushing up against my thigh. I want to ask him to move back, but I don't. Officer Chin is on the opposite side of the long table, glaring at me like I shot somebody.

"So, Graylin, do you know why you're here?" Officer Chin asks.

"Nope," I mumble. Then I hear my grandmother's voice. She's old school and is always telling me to be respectful to adults. "I mean, no, sir."

I don't like looking at the Asian cop. If they try a good-cop, bad-cop act on me, he's probably going to play the bad cop.

"First, I need to tell you that you're in some major trouble," the mean one says.

I've already decided that's what I'm going to call Officer Chin—Mean Cop—because that's what he is.

I don't say anything since he hasn't asked me a question.

"How old are you?"

"Fourteen."

"Your principal got a report that you have a naked picture of one of your classmates on your phone."

"But I don't." *Not anymore.*

"Do you know Kennedy Carlyle?"

"Yes."

"Is she your girlfriend?"

I screw up my face. "No." Kennedy is way too stuck-up to be anybody's girlfriend.

"Well, how do you know her?"

"She's in my English and algebra classes."

I don't want to talk to them because I know they aren't on my side. I watch a lot of crime shows on TV with my granny. The cops always act like they want to help you, but they'd rather shoot a black kid than help him. They just need to read me my rights and—*Oh snap!* I suddenly remember what my dad told me to do if the police ever stopped me.

I sit up straight and try to look brave. "My dad told me not to talk to the police without his permission."

Mean Cop rolls his eyes. "Is that right? Does your daddy know you have a naked picture of one of your classmates on your phone?"

*But I don't.* I want to smile, but I know that will get me in even more trouble.

Mean Cop grips the edge of the table and leans forward. "If I were you, I'd want to defend myself. So, if you want us to hear your side of the story, you better start talking."

I don't know what to do. I want to defend myself, but my dad gave me strict instructions. *If a cop stops you, don't say a damn word.*

Officer Fenton bumps my thigh with his knee again, which makes me flinch. "Look, Graylin, we need you to be honest with us. If you do, we can cut you some slack."

Even though I wish he wouldn't sit so close to me, at least he talks nice to me. Still, I keep quiet.

"According to the report we received," Mean Cop continues, "you've been going all over the school showing people a naked picture of Kennedy Carlyle."

Before I can stop myself, I blurt out, "No, I didn't! Somebody's lying on me!"

Of course, I'd *planned* to show the picture to my best friend Crayvon, but you can't go to jail for something you were only thinking about doing.

"If you have the picture on your phone," Officer Fenton says, "just be truthful about it and we'll see what we can do to keep you out of trouble."

They must think I'm stupid. I do what my dad told me to do and keep my mouth shut.

Mean Cop pounds the table with his fist, making me jump two inches out of my chair. "Where's your phone?"

I still don't answer. Everybody has the right to remain silent, even kids.

"I said where's your phone?" Mean Cop repeats.

I hide my hands underneath the table so he can't see them shaking.

Officer Fenton pats me on the shoulder. "C'mon, Graylin, you seem like a good kid. I bet you make good grades, don't you?"

I nod and start to tell them I got honors certificates in math and science last year, but I figure they still won't let me go. "My dad"—I start to stutter—"my dad told me not to talk to the police without his permission."

"Why don't you help us out here?" Officer Fenton says. "We really need to see your phone. We'll take a quick look and if there's no picture, we'll send you back to class."

A squeaky voice comes out of my mouth. "It's…it's in my backpack."

As soon as the words are out, I want to kick myself. Now I've just lied to the police. Again.

"And where's your backpack?"

"In my locker."

"Why don't we go with you to your locker so you can get it?" Officer Fenton says.

"My dad told me not to talk to the police without his permission," I say for the third time.

Officer Fenton frowns. "This is a very serious matter, son."

Mean Cop thumps his fingers on the table. "Why don't you just—"

The voice of Young Thug singing *RiRi* fills the room.

*Ah-ah-ah work*
*Do the work baby do the work*
*Tonight baby do the work baby do the work.*

When I hear my ringtone, my stomach lurches up into my throat. I'm about to throw up the oatmeal I had for breakfast.

Mean Cop scrunches up his face like a WWE wrestler. "Did your daddy also teach you to lie to the police? Give me the damn phone!"

I shakily pull it from my pocket and set it on the table.

Officer Fenton picks it up, taps the screen, then looks over at me. "What's the password?"

I stare down at the table.

"I said what's the password?" Now he's turning mean too.

"LeBron forty-three."

"For your sake, young man, I hope you're telling us the truth."

After a couple of minutes, Officer Fenton looks at Mean Cop and shakes his head. "Nothing in his photos or texts. I only see a few recent emails. Nothing there either." He sets the phone back on the table.

Mean Cop grunts. "Let me look." He stretches one of his short arms across the table and grabs my phone.

He taps the screen a few times, then starts smiling. "Well, well, well, what do we have here? Looks like you forgot to check his deleted pictures, partner."

Mean Cop holds up my phone and shows me the picture I thought was gone forever. A warm trickle of pee runs down my left leg.

"You're quite the little liar, aren't you?" Mean Cop yells at me. "Where're the rest of the pictures?"

"There aren't any more," I stutter. "That was the only one I had."

"Did you take it?"

"No."

"You lied about your phone being in your locker, you lied about having this picture, and you're still lying now!"

"My...my dad"—I can't get my words out—"my dad told me not to talk to the police without his permission."

"When your daddy told you that, he didn't realize you'd be in this kind of trouble. If you didn't take this picture, how'd it get on your phone?"

"Somebody sent it to me."

"Who?"

"I don't know."

My throat hurts and it feels like somebody's pressing down on my chest. If the table wasn't in the way, I'd hug my knees to my chest.

Mean Cop pulls out his handcuffs and dangles them from his finger. "Stop lying and tell us the truth," he barks. "If you don't, you're going to jail."

# CHAPTER 4

## *Gus*

"The police?" I shoot to my feet so fast the chair topples backward, banging into the wall. "Like hell he is! They can't talk to my son without my permission. Take me to him. Now!"

I hear yelling coming from the door to my right. Before the principal can stop me, I burst into the room.

"What the hell!" My son is in handcuffs, a white cop gripping him by the forearm.

"Dad! Dad! Please help me!" Graylin cries. "Dad, please don't let them arrest me!"

I charge up to the cop holding Graylin. "What are you doing to my son?"

"Sir, you need to calm down," yells an Asian cop. He extends his right palm toward me while his other hand grazes the butt of his gun. "Please back up, sir!"

I defiantly stay put. "I asked you what you're doing to my son. You can't interrogate him without my permission."

"I told you to step back!" the Asian cop yells, twice as loud as before.

When I still don't move, he snatches his Beretta from its holster and points it at me. "I said back up! Now!"

"Oh my God!" the principal cries. "Please, Mr. Alexander. Please step back!"

"Dad, Dad, please go back!" Graylin's sobbing hysterically now. "They're going to shoot you. I'm okay! Please, Dad, go back! Please!"

The *only* reason I take two small steps backward is because the cop's hand is so unsteady I fear he might actually shoot me. But I'm way madder than he is nervous.

The cop lowers his gun but doesn't return it to the holster.

Heat stings my face. "What are you doing to my son?"

"Sir, you need to lower your voice," says the cop restraining Graylin.

"You can't talk to him without my permission."

"We don't need your permission," he says.

"Please, Dad!" Graylin cries. "It's okay! I'll be okay. Please, Dad! I don't want them to shoot you! Please do what they say!"

The Asian cop looks past me at the principal. "We found the picture."

Principal Keller gasps and cups her mouth.

I'm so pissed off my vision is blurry. But it's my son's terror-stricken face, not the Beretta still in that cop's hand that forces me to regain control of my senses. I take a few more steps back, lower my voice, but amplify my outrage.

"Why is my son in handcuffs?"

The Asian cop eyes me with contempt. "Because he's under arrest."

"For what?"

"Possession of child pornography."

# CHAPTER 5

## Graylin

*Possession of child pornography?*

"What?" I cry out. "I don't have any child pornography!"

Principal Keller looks just as shocked as me and my dad. She's hugging herself and rubbing her hands up and down her arms.

*This is all your fault! Why'd you call the police on me?*

My dad backs up all the way into Principal Keller's office and Mean Cop finally puts his gun away.

"Please, Dad, don't let them take me to jail!" My face is wet with tears and snot. "I swear I didn't do anything wrong. I swear, I didn't!"

My dad's fists are clenched tight, which is how I know he's really, really mad.

"I can bring him down to the police station," he says. "You don't have to arrest him."

Officer Fenton pulls me past my dad into the main office. Once we're outside in the hallway, it seems like half the school has lined up for a parade. As the cops march me toward the front entrance of the school, everyone stares and points at me.

*"What happened?"*

*"What did Graylin do?"*

*"Graylin's too smart to get arrested."*

I glance back over my shoulder and I'm relieved to see my dad following us.

They tug me down the steps to a police car parked in front of the school. Officer Fenton opens the back door, palms the top of my head like a basketball and pushes me into the seat.

My dad moves toward me, but Mean Cop grips the butt of his gun. "You need to stay back, sir, and let us do our jobs."

I'm crying so hard I feel like I might throw up.

"Where are you taking him?" My dad's voice sounds muffled through the thick car window.

"Eastlake Juvenile Hall," Officer Fenton says. "They'll call you."

"Can I go with him? He's just a kid. He's only fourteen."

"It doesn't work like that."

The two cops climb into the front and slam the doors. As I stare up at my dad, the unbelievable sight in front of me sends a chill through my whole body. Tears are streaming down my dad's face. I've never seen my dad cry. When my Uncle Diddy got shot, I thought my dad was going to cry, but he didn't. Not even at the funeral. So I didn't think my dad *could* cry.

As the car pulls away from the curb, he starts jogging alongside it.

"I'm coming to get you!" my dad yells. "Don't talk to them! Don't say nothing to nobody!"

# CHAPTER 6

## *Simone*

As soon as the plane touches down at LAX, I unbuckle my seatbelt. I can't wait to show my daughter Kennedy the new cell phone cover I bought her on my business trip to New York. She'll be the only eighth grader at snooty Marcus Prep with real diamonds on her phone.

I take my phone out of airplane mode and it instantly starts pinging with text messages.

I'm the first one to step into the jetway. I'm reading a text from my assistant when my phone rings.

"Hello, Mrs. Carlyle. This is Gloria Keller. From Marcus Preparatory Academy."

I stop cold, forcing the man behind me to swerve left as he curses under his breath.

"Oh my God! What's the matter? Is Kennedy okay? What happened?"

"Kennedy's fine."

I instantly relax, a little embarrassed about my panicked reaction. She's probably calling about a donation. "You don't have to ask," I tell her. "We're good for five grand for the Spring fundraiser."

"That's not why I'm calling. We've had an incident."

The click-clacking of my pink Jimmy Choos on the airport tile abruptly stops. "What do you mean by *an incident*?"

I hear Keller suck in a gulp of air. "We received an anonymous report that one of our male students had an inappropriate picture of Kennedy on his cell phone."

For the next few seconds it's as if someone has pressed a mute button, silencing the airport's background noise.

"What kind of inappropriate picture?"

"Well, um, a naked picture."

"How did he get a naked picture of my baby?"

"I have no idea. The police have arrested him."

"What's his name?"

"I'm not at liberty to provide that information. He's a minor and—"

"If some boy is sending naked pictures of my baby all over that school, I have a right to know his name."

"Please, Mrs. Carlyle, calm down. The report only mentioned one picture, not multiple pictures. And we don't have any information that he sent it to anyone."

"I don't care if it's one or ten." I drop my professionalism and use words that more accurately convey my disgust. "I put my child in that school because I didn't want her exposed to a bunch of ghetto-ass hood rats. I can't believe you let this happen. And just so you know, I'm suing that little pervert, his parents, *and* the school."

# CHAPTER 7

## *Graylin*

The backseat of the police cruiser smells like the bums that sleep outside the Quickstop Liquor Store on Manchester. And that makes me want to throw up.

"We're here." Mean Cop glances back at me as the police car rolls to a stop. Two giant steel gates slowly open and I can't help thinking we're driving into a dungeon.

Mean Cop opens the back door, grabs my arm and pulls me from the car. It's hard to keep my balance with my hands cuffed behind my back. I dip my head and try to wipe the snot off my nose with my shoulder, but Mean Cop acts like I'm trying to escape and squeezes my arm real hard.

They walk me inside where three men are standing behind bulletproof windows like at the bank. Mean Cop walks up to the counter, spouts off my name and starts filling out some paperwork.

A gruff-looking Mexican man steps out from behind the counter. "I'll take it from here. Take off the cuffs."

Mean Cop unlocks my handcuffs. "He's all yours."

"I'm Mr. Cardoza," the man says, as I massage my sore wrists. "I'm a detention services officer." I'm glad he's talking nice to me. "I'm going to explain the rules to you, okay?"

I nod as he starts patting me down.

"I'll need you to answer *yes* or *no* so I know you understand me, okay?"

I nod again. "I mean, yes, sir."

"This your first time here?"

"Yes, sir."

"I thought so."

"So is this the jail?"

He smiles. "No, this isn't a jail. This is Eastlake Juvenile Hall. Take a look at that sign." Mr. Cardoza points at a poster on the wall. "Can you read?"

"Yes. I get mostly A's."

"That's good." He gives me a wink. "Take a few minutes to look over the rules, then we'll read them together."

I'm a fast reader, so it doesn't take me long to read all 15 of them, which are in English and Spanish. No profanity, no gang slogans, no fighting or horse playing, no weapons or drugs, and no loud talking. A couple of them seem kind of lame, like no sex talk, mother talk, escape talk or race talk.

Mr. Cardoza spends another 10 minutes going over the rules one by one. There's no way I can remember all of them. Since I never do that kind of stuff, I don't even try.

Mr. Cardoza uses a key on his belt to unlock a door and leads me down a long hallway.

"Where are we going?"

"To the Boys Receiving Unit."

I want to ask what that is, but I don't. I hope it's not like it is on *Lockup* where you have to take off all your clothes and bend over so a guard can look inside your butt.

"Um, do I get a phone call? I want to call my dad."

"Sure, as soon as we get you processed."

That makes me so happy I almost start crying again. I'm surprised that juvenile hall looks a lot like my old elementary school. Everything is beige and old with lots of windows. They even have grass and plants. We stop near an open doorway where a black woman is sitting behind a desk. She reminds me of my aunt Macie because of her dark skin and short hair. All of the staff, including Mr. Cardoza, are dressed in beige khakis and dark-blue golf shirts. Since they don't have guns, maybe this really isn't a jail.

"This is Graylin Alexander," Mr. Cardoza says. "A first-timer. He's an A student."

The woman smiles at me. "I'm Ms. Turner. Here's your towel roll. You need to shower and change into the clothes wrapped inside that towel." She points at a man standing a few feet away. "Mr. Winston handles the boys."

I wish Ms. Turner could stay with me, but I'm too afraid to ask her to.

I look through a big window and see two gangbanger-looking boys sitting on a bench. One of them has tattoos all over his shaved head.

"The showers are over there," Mr. Winston says.

He points to a gray cemented area with four shower stalls that don't have any doors. I put my towel roll on a bench underneath a small window. When Mr. Winston doesn't move, I realize he's going to stand there and watch me.

"Let's go. We don't have all day."

I unwrap the towel roll and find a white T-shirt, briefs, socks, gray sweatpants and a gray sweatshirt. Turning my back to Mr. Winston, I pull my shirt over my head, then strip off my underwear, which reeks of urine.

They didn't give me a face towel, so I guess I have to use my hands. I take several pumps from a soap dispenser outside the shower stall and step inside. The warm water feels good and I want to stay here forever.

"That's long enough," Mr. Winston says, after only a few minutes.

I step out of the shower and run over to the bench to grab my towel. Our bathroom at home has a heater, which I miss right now because it's freezing cold. I quickly dry myself off with the towel, which isn't thick and soft like the ones we have at home. I always put on deodorant and Vaseline after getting out of the shower, but I guess they don't have any here.

After I'm dressed in my sweatshirt and sweatpants, Ms. Turner asks me a bunch of questions.

*No*, I don't take any medications. *No*, I don't have any allergies. *No*, I don't have asthma or seizures or lice. *No*, I'm not autistic and *no* I don't have any mental conditions or health issues like ADD. After what seems like fifty more questions, she leads me down another hallway to an office with two desks that seem too big for such a little room. A man with an afro stands up and shakes my hand.

"I'm Mr. Jackson. What's your full name?"

"Graylin Michael Alexander."

"Okay, Graylin, have a seat. I'm your detention and control officer. You'll also be assigned a probation officer."

*Probation officer? I haven't even had a trial yet. How can I be on probation already?*

I know my dad told me not to talk to anybody, but I have to ask. "Why do I have a probation officer? I haven't even been convicted of anything."

Mr. Jackson laughs. "Every kid gets assigned a probation officer. I'll explain how it works in a second."

"The other man"—I try to remember his name but I can't— "the one who told me all the rules said I could call my dad."

"You sure can. I have a few things to go over with you first."

Mr. Jackson types something into his computer, then turns back to me. He tells me that the police arrested me for possession of child pornography, California Penal Code 311.1, then he starts reading me my rights.

"You have the right to remain silent," he begins. "Anything you say can and will be used against you in a court of law..."

I'm mad because Mean Cop should've read me my rights before they took me in that conference room. Then I wouldn't have said anything or given them my phone. The words sound just like they do on TV, which makes me want to start crying again because I'm not a criminal.

"Do you understand the rights I've just read to you?"

"Yes, sir." I'm not too sure I understood everything, only the part about being silent.

"Would you like to speak with me?"

I can hear my dad yelling at me through the window of the police car, telling me not to talk to anybody. But Mr. Jackson is being so nice to me, I don't want to make him mad.

"Um, no, sir." I try to sound respectful so he won't get upset. "I want to be silent."

"This is a chance for you to tell me your side of the story. Are you sure you don't want to speak with me about what happened at school?"

I *do* want to explain everything to him so he can let me go home. But I have to do what my dad told me to do.

"My dad told me not to talk to anybody."

"Okay, that's fine."

I'm glad Mr. Jackson doesn't seem mad. Now he starts asking me almost as many questions as Ms. Turner.

I tell him the name of my school, my age, my grade, my birthdate, my address. *No,* I'm not a foster kid. *No,* I don't have a social worker. *No,* I've never been arrested or suspended from school or picked up for truancy.

Then he starts asking me about my family. I tell him that I'm an only child, that I live with my dad and my granny, and that my mama is on drugs and we don't know where she is.

"Do your father or grandmother drink alcohol in the home?"

That question makes me kinda nervous. "Only my dad. But he never gets drunk."

"What about drugs?"

"My dad and my granny don't do drugs. Just my mama."

"What about weed? Does your dad smoke weed?"

My dad has never smoked weed in front of me, but I've smelled it on him a couple of times. I don't want to lie again, but if I tell the truth, my dad could get in trouble. Maybe if I hadn't lied about that picture, they wouldn't have arrested me. Then I remember that weed is legal in California now. It's the same as drinking alcohol, so they can't arrest my dad for that.

"Um, I think my dad smokes weed, but not in front of me."

I expect Mr. Jackson to look surprised, but he just moves on to the next question.

My head is hurting by the time I finish giving him my whole life story. Then he goes over the same rules the other officer made me read, even though I told him we already did that.

"Can I call my dad now?" I ask when we're done.

"Sure." Mr. Jackson picks up the telephone receiver from his desk. "What's his number?"

My mind goes as blank as a computer screen. I always call my dad from the *Favorites* on my phone. I try to concentrate, but his number won't come to me. I can't even remember my home number so I can talk to my granny.

"I don't know my dad's number." Tears start falling again and my chest is hurting now. "It's…it's in my phone."

Without my phone, I don't know *anybody's* number.

# CHAPTER 8

## Angela

Most people hate being stuck in traffic, but I welcome the downtime. I actually feel a sense of Zen as my car moves along at a snail's pace

My phone rings and I smile when I see that it's my boyfriend Dre.

When I pick up, his words come at me like he's firing them from a machine gun.

"Dre, slow down. I can't understand a word you're saying."

"Graylin got arrested!"

Dre and Graylin's father are best friends. Graylin even calls him Uncle Dre.

"Arrested? For what?"

As Dre explains the situation, I feel my stomach clench. Just a few months ago, Dre rescued his 13-year-old niece Brianna from sex traffickers. Now this.

"They took him to juvenile hall. We have to go down there and get him out."

"Which one?" There are at least three juvenile facilities in the L.A. area.

"Eastlake. Gus is with me. We're headed there now."

I make a left on LaBrea and head for the Santa Monica Freeway. "I'm on my way."

As soon as I'm on the freeway, I get to work on something Gus hasn't yet asked me to do—finding legal representation for Graylin.

Since I practice criminal defense in addition to employment law, Gus will probably want me to handle Graylin's case. But my practice is almost exclusively in state and federal court. Juvenile court has totally different rules and I don't speak the language.

I call a couple of friends and ask them to recommend a top-notch juvenile defense attorney. "I want the attorney you'd hire to represent your kid," I tell them.

Within twenty minutes, both of them call back with three names. Only one name appears on both lists: Jenny Ungerman.

After getting Gus' okay, I give Jenny a call. When I start gushing over her reputation, she abruptly waves off the praise. "Tell me what's going on."

She listens to the few facts I can provide, then sighs long and hard.

"Don't worry. Graylin's father can pay your fee." I'm not sure that's true since I haven't asked about her rates.

"That sigh wasn't reluctance to take the case. It was frustration. So far this year, I've had eight cases where the D.A.'s office went after kids for sexting."

"That many?"

"Yep. And they're not just charging kids with possession and distribution of child pornography, they're actually locking them up. My last client, who was fifteen, got a year for convincing his girlfriend to pose nude and then sending her picture to his best friend, who put it on Instagram. It ultimately ended up on some underground pedophile site."

"You couldn't plead it down to a lesser charge?"

"I tried, but the asshole D.A. wouldn't budge. Prosecutors have a lot of discretion as to who gets charged. Some of them read the statutes literally and will go after anyone in possession of a naked picture of a kid, even if it's another kid."

I pray to God Graylin hasn't taken a naked picture of some girl. "So will you take the case?"

"Yes, of course. It'll take me about forty minutes to get down to Eastlake."

"Thanks. It sounds like Graylin might be in some serious trouble."

"If he has a naked picture of an underage girl on his phone, there's no *might* about it," Jenny says. "These days, a smartphone in the hands of a kid can have more devastating consequences than giving them a loaded gun. And the average parent doesn't have a clue."

# CHAPTER 9

## *Simone*

I charge through the front door of our home like I'm there to put out a fire. Kennedy's in the den, sitting on the couch next to her father.

"My baby!" I call out, pulling her into my arms. Her eyes are puffy and her bangs are matted to her forehead. "I'm so sorry this had to happen to you."

"Oh, Mommy, I'm so embarrassed. LaShay says everybody at school is talking about the picture. I'm never going back to that school again!"

Percy peers down at Kennedy. "Honey, we need to talk about what happened. Was this kid your boyfriend or something?"

"Boyfriend?" I scream. "Percy, you know darn well Kennedy's not allowed to date until she's sixteen."

Percy pats Kennedy on the shoulder. "Everything's going to be fine, sweetie. But I don't understand how that boy got a naked picture of you? Do you even know him?"

I pull Kennedy closer. "How in the world would she know how he got it? He's probably some pervert."

"Please turn off the drama machine for a second, Simone. Okay? I'm just trying to get to the bottom of this."

"His name's Graylin Alexander, Daddy. He's in two of my classes. I don't know how he got my picture. I promise."

"Where was the picture taken?" Percy asks.

"I don't know," Kennedy sniffs. "LaShay said they arrested him because he had it on his phone. Daddy, I'm so embarrassed!"

"Sweetie, you know you can tell us anything, right," Percy continues to push. "You haven't let some boy take pictures of you, have you?"

"Percy! Are you out of your mind?"

"Look, Simone, we have to ask. One of my law partners found out his daughter was sexting a boy at her school. She was only a year older than Kennedy."

"What that little fast girl did has nothing to do with my child."

"No, Daddy. I didn't sext anybody, I promise. Can I go back to my room now? My head hurts."

As Kennedy leaves, I light into Percy. "Why in the world would you interrogate your own child like she's some hostile witness?"

Percy rubs his forehead. "I'm just trying to understand how this could've happened. Maybe it's a fake picture. Her head on somebody else's body. That's pretty easy to do on a computer."

"Whether it's fake or not, we're suing that school, that boy and his parents."

"We're going to handle this," Percy says. "But let's not make a federal case out of it."

My head rears back like a stunned cobra. "What did you say?"

"Let's wait until we have all the facts. I'm not sure suing anybody is the best thing for Kennedy."

"Oh, this is interesting. Mr. Big Time Lawyer sues people every day of the week, but wants to run and hide when his daughter's reputation is on the line."

"My daughter's reputation is *exactly* what I'm thinking about. A lawsuit means publicity and publicity will only cause more embarrassment for Kennedy. We need to address this quickly and quietly. Can we please focus on what's best for our daughter rather than your penchant for payback?"

"I guess you also expect me to sit back and do nothing while you continue screwing your little associate."

Percy stands up. "I've told you a thousand times, I'm not seeing anybody. Jesus Christ! Your constant badgering me over this nonsense is exactly why I left."

My husband moved out three months ago claiming we'd *grown apart*. Although he won't admit it, I know he's having an affair.

"We should put her in a new school," Percy says.

"I don't want her at *any* school right now. We can home-school her."

His brow arches. "Really? So you're going to be around to do that?"

"You're not going to make me feel guilty for having a career. We can pay someone to come in."

"That's just like you. Job first, family second."

"How dare you—"

Like always, Percy is out of the door before I've had a chance to say my piece. I hate the way he so easily dismisses me.

I grab my cell phone and start scrolling through my contacts. We're major campaign donors and have a ton of important political connections. I'm about to call in some favors.

That little hoodlum Graylin Alexander deserves to be in jail for what he did to my child. And I'm going to do everything in my power to make sure that's exactly where he ends up.

# CHAPTER 10

## *Angela*

Thirty minutes and two wrong turns later, I finally make it to Eastlake Juvenile Hall. The only parking spot I can find is almost a block away.

From a quick Google search, I learn that Eastlake—also referred to as Central Juvenile Hall—sits on more than twenty acres in the Boyle Heights section of Los Angeles. It's the oldest youth detention center in the country, established back in 1912. Most of its residents are black and Hispanic. Only about twenty percent are female.

A security guard waves me through a metal detector, while a different one checks my purse. I'm barely inside the tiny lobby before Gus and Dre rush up to me.

I give Gus a hug as I squeeze Dre's hand. Gus has a muscular build and is just under six feet. He and Dre did time together at Corcoran State Prison. Since then, they've both committed to a crime-free life and now team up rehabbing houses.

"Jenny should be here any minute. She'll explain how everything works and get us in to see Graylin."

Just then, a tall, slim white woman with shoulder-length auburn hair steps through the metal detectors. As she heads our way, she walks with a lawyer's confidence and has the polished prettiness of a TV news anchor.

"Are you Angela Evans?" the woman asks.

I nod. "And you must be Jenny Ungerman. Thanks so much for getting here so quickly."

Jenny's wide brown eyes and pert smile convey a friendly, easygoing vibe. After short introductions, we all sit down and Gus starts bombarding her with questions.

"How soon can we post bail and get him outta here? And why were those cops talking to him without my permission? I don't understand how—"

Jenny raises her hands. "Mr. Alexander, I know you're concerned about your son. But we need to discuss a few things before we proceed."

Gus sighs, then nods.

"First, my retainer to handle Graylin's case through adjudication is twenty thousand dollars. If there are any special hearings, it could be more."

Dre and Gus pin me with a stupefied look that says, *This chick is all about the money.* But Jenny is doing what she has to do. When you're a defense attorney, your fee has to be the first order of business. If the client can't afford you, there's no need for any further discussion. Attorneys don't work for free, especially not the good ones.

"What's adjudi—what's that mean?" Gus asks.

"That's what a trial is called in the juvenile system."

Jenny's fee is a little on the high side, but not outrageous.

"Would you be willing to accept a small retainer, and the rest via monthly payments?" I ask.

"As a professional courtesy to you, I'll do that. But I'll need a cashier's check for five thousand dollars before making my first court appearance."

I pull Gus and Dre off to the side. "Twenty friggin' grand?" Gus says. "Are you kidding me?"

"Can't he get a public defender?" Dre asks. "It ain't like he's facing a felony or something."

"I know some great public defenders, but you don't get to choose the one you want," I tell them. "From everything I've been told, Jenny's worth every penny."

"I'll kick in," Dre says to Gus. "And I know your sister Macie will too."

Once Gus tells Jenny he'd like to proceed, she pulls a retainer agreement from her satchel and says he should review it and call her if he has any questions.

"Now, to your questions," Jenny begins. "First, there's no bail for juveniles."

Gus' forehead creases. "I can't bail him out? How long will he have to stay here?"

"The lack of a bail system is a good thing. Unless a kid is accused of a violent crime, has trouble at home or a prior record, he'll usually be released to a parent or guardian."

Gus leans back in his chair and exhales. "So I can get him out of here tonight. Thank God."

"I didn't say that," Jenny says. "We won't know for sure until I speak with one of the detention officers."

"Graylin's a good kid," I say, hoping to reduce some of Gus' anxiety. "I'm sure they'll let him come home."

Jenny fixes me with a scorching glare that I don't quite understand. This is Graylin we're talking about. He's a model child. Of course they're going to let him go home.

"What I wanna know," Gus says, "is why those cops were interrogating my son without my permission. They should've—"

"The police don't need parental consent to question a minor in California."

This time, Dre speaks up. "For real?"

"That's always a shock to parents," Jenny says. "And the school also doesn't need probable cause to search him, just reasonable suspicion."

She turns to Gus. "Mr. Alexander, I need to explain something else that's sometimes a little difficult for parents to understand. Even though Graylin's a minor, if you hire me to represent him, he's my client, not you."

Gus cocks his head. "And what exactly does that mean?"

Jenny forces a smile. "It means that even though you'll be paying my bill, my only obligation is to Graylin. I can keep you updated about the case, but only to the extent Graylin allows me to do so. And to be completely clear, I'll be following Graylin's directions, not yours."

Both Gus and Dre look over at me as if I'm pranking them.

"That's nuts," Dre says. "Graylin's just a kid."

I jump in to head off a confrontation. "Let's just listen to everything she has to say. What else, Jenny?"

"You shouldn't ask Graylin anything about his case. There's a privilege between a husband and wife, but not between a parent and child. If Graylin admits something incriminating, you could be compelled to testify against him."

The creases in Gus' forehead deepen into crevices. "Lady, don't talk to me like I'm stupid. Even if Graylin did tell me something, I'd never testify against my own son."

Jenny shows no reaction to Gus' hostile tone. She's obviously done this dance before. "I can't allow you to lie under oath, Mr. Alexander. So, it's best that you don't have any knowledge of the underlying facts."

"Are you saying I can't even ask him if he did what they're accusing him of?"

"Yes, that's exactly what I'm saying."

Gus glares at me again. "And this is who you want to represent my son?"

I place a hand on Gus' forearm. "Let's just get Graylin out of here and take it from there."

Jenny stands up. "Let me go see if I can make that happen."

We stand in a huddle for another twenty minutes or so before Jenny returns. The stern look on her face telegraphs that she doesn't have good news.

"I'm sorry, but they're keeping him here until his arraignment and detention hearing. A judge will have to decide whether he can go home."

Gus' face tightens with tension. "And when is that going to happen?"

Jenny pauses. "Detention hearings have to be held within forty-eight hours of arrest, not counting weekends. Since this is Friday, he probably won't see the judge until Tuesday."

"Are you kidding me?" Gus shouts. "He has to stay here for four friggin' days!"

In seconds, the security guard darts across the lobby and is standing only inches from Gus. "Is there a problem here? You'll need to keep your voice down, sir."

"I'm sorry, officer," Jenny says with a stiff smile. "Everything's fine. I had to give this father some disappointing news about his son and he's understandably upset. We'll keep it down."

Gus rubs his forehead.

"Why are they keeping him?" I ask. "What happened?"

"When a kid is charged with certain crimes, remaining in custody until the detention hearing is mandatory. They've added a second charge." She briefly looks away. "Making a criminal threat."

Gus slumps into the nearest chair and doesn't say a word.

Dre blinks several times. "What criminal threat?"

"An anonymous note started all of this. It said Graylin threatened to beat the girl up and embarrass her by putting her picture on Instagram."

"I know my kid," Gus says. "And that's not him. How can they lock him up based on some anonymous note?"

"Like I said," Dre repeats through clenched teeth, "what criminal threat?"

"I know it sounds crazy," Jenny continues, her tone apologetic, "but in this day and age of sensitivity about bullying, when a kid threatens to beat up somebody and embarrass them on social media, it's considered a criminal threat under the California Penal Code."

Nobody says a word. Jenny wisely gives us a few seconds to let this sink in.

"But I do have some good news for you, Mr. Alexander." Jenny smiles for the first time as Gus slowly raises his head.

"They're going to let you see him. In fact, Graylin's waiting for you right now."

# CHAPTER 11

## *Miguel*

I listen to the voicemail message from my boss and high-five the air. I'm about to be called up to the big leagues.

I've only been a juvenile prosecutor for eight months, but it's not uncommon for the shinning stars—like me—to get promoted to adult court on the fast track. Unlike most of my colleagues, I come in early, stay late, deal with the political crap and never complain when I have to take over a case another deputy D.A. screwed up.

Walking in long, proud strides, I head for the elevators with a serious pep in my step. I have the thin, taut body of a long-distance runner because I am one, logging more than forty miles a week. I wear boxy black glasses I don't actually need in a deliberate effort to appear older than my thirty-one years.

"Have a seat, Martinez," my boss says when I knock on his open door.

Deputy-in-Charge Sol Stein is a chubby-faced man with graying hair and a portly build. He never wastes time on small talk.

"We have another sexting case," Stein says, scratching his balding crown. "It's a wobbler, but file it as a felony, not a misdemeanor."

My jaw goes slack as my dream of a promotion dissipates like a puff of smoke. *Not another sexting case.*

"And why are we filing it as a felony?"

"This boy made the mistake of getting caught with a naked picture of a girl whose father and mother are close to the mayor."

"Who're the parents?"

Stein pulls a piece of paper from one of the messy piles on his desk. "The father's Percy Carlyle, a partner at Morgan Lewis. The mother, Simone Carlyle, is a V.P. at AT&T. Their daughter and the boy—Graylin Alexander—were classmates at Marcus Preparatory Academy."

Marcus Prep is a well-regarded private school. "White victim?" I ask, assuming she is.

"Nope. Black. The boy too."

"How old are they?"

"Both fourteen."

"Did the boy convince the girl to strip for him?"

"Don't know. The police confiscated his phone with the girl's picture on it. So it's an open-and-shut case for possession. You'll need to see how the evidence plays out on distribution. No telling who he sent it to."

"Is it a boyfriend-girlfriend thing?"

"I don't have any other facts," Stein says. "We need to make a public example of this kid. Maybe hearing about the case will force other parents to start monitoring what their children are doing online."

*What a load of crap.* This is about politics and payola. The girl's angry parents called the mayor, the mayor called the D.A., and the D.A. called Stein.

As I stand up, a rancid feeling swirls like a tornado in the pit of my stomach. I've prosecuted my share of teenage thugs who were as hardcore as any convict at San Quentin, but kids who take naked selfies aren't criminals and I hate throwing the book at them. I'm almost at the door when I decide to say what's on my mind.

"It's crazy for us to bring these kids up on pornography charges. If I'd had a camera phone when I was fourteen, I would've been taking pictures of my girlfriend's boobs too."

Stein chuckles. "I didn't write the laws. Until the state legislature does something about it, it's our job to prosecute these brats."

# CHAPTER 12

### *Angela*

When Jenny and Gus start following a staff member into the facility, I fall in step behind them, but the security guard stops me.

"Only parents and attorneys. You his mother?"

"No. His attorney."

A hint of a frown glazes Jenny's lips.

"Can I see your bar card and driver's license?" the guard asks.

He glances at them, then hands me something to sign.

The guy takes us from the waiting area down a wide hallway. Gus is looking the place up and down, from the beige walls to the gray linoleum floor tiles. Except for the locked doors, the place has the feel of a school, not a jail or a prison. We walk past a wall with motivational words stenciled in English and Spanish. *Respecto. Respect. Orgullo. Pride. Sobresalga. Excel.*

We're taken to a small oblong room inside the Boys Receiving Unit. It looks more like a storage closet than an office. A minute later, the door opens and Graylin flies into his father's arms.

"Dad, please get me out of here! They're lying on me. I'm innocent!"

"I know, Little Man, I know." Gus pulls him close. "Don't worry. We're gonna get you outta here. I promise."

Graylin's a beefy kid with a round, innocent face.

"Can I go home with you? Please, Dad. I don't wanna stay here!"

Jenny and I stand with our backs to the door while Gus and Graylin remain locked in an embrace.

"We only have a few minutes," Jenny says. "I'd like to go over a few things with Graylin." She offers her hand to him. "My name is Jenny Ungerman. I'm your attorney. Your dad hired me to represent you."

Graylin squints as if he just realized we were in the room. "How come Ms. Angela can't be my attorney?"

"Jenny's an expert in juvenile cases," I explain. "But I'll be helping out as well."

Jenny's tightly pursed lips tell me she's not thrilled about what I just said. My words are as much of a surprise to me as they are to her. I hadn't planned on participating in Graylin's defense until the words spilled out of my mouth.

"You're not going to be able to go home tonight," Jenny explains. "The judge won't decide that until Tuesday."

Graylin whips his head in his father's direction. "I have to stay here all the way to Tuesday?" His voice crumples. "How come I can't go home with you? Can't you bail me out?"

Gus pulls him close again. "I know this is hard, but I need you to man up. Just do what Ms. Jenny says and everything's going to be okay."

"It's very important that you don't talk to anyone about your case," Jenny says firmly. "That includes other kids you meet in here. Absolutely no one, except me."

*And me,* I want to add.

"Not even my dad?"

"Not even your dad. If you tell somebody something about your case, even your dad, they could be forced to testify about what you told them in court. Even if you tell it to them in secret. So it's very important that you don't say *anything* to *anybody* about what happened. Do you understand?"

Graylin nods weakly. "I understand. The police put snitches in your jail cell to try to make you incriminate yourself."

"That's right," Jenny says.

"And I want you to understand that you're my client, not your dad. Even though your dad may be paying me, you make the decisions about your case, not anyone else. Do you have any questions?"

Graylin pauses like he expects his dad to object.

"Um, aren't you going to ask me what happened so I can show you I'm innocent?"

"I'll be back tomorrow afternoon to meet with you. You can explain everything to me then."

"Can my dad come to our meeting?"

"Your father can visit you tomorrow," Jenny says, "but for our first meeting, I only want to meet with you. Your dad can attend future meetings as long as that's okay with you."

Gus scratches his jaw and looks away.

"Five more minutes," says a voice from outside the door.

Graylin hugs his dad even tighter.

"We'll let you two have these last few minutes alone," Jenny says.

I follow her into the hallway.

"I didn't realize this would be a two-member defense team," Jenny says, the instant the door is closed. "

"I didn't either until I said it. But I think I'd like to be involved in Graylin's defense."

"Well, I guess we'll just have to see."

*We'll just have to see?* "Yes," I reply. "We will."

# CHAPTER 13

## *Graylin*

I don't know how I'm going to survive in here for four whole days. And I still don't understand how they can put somebody in jail when you haven't done anything wrong. As soon as I find out who sent me that picture, I'm going to make sure my attorneys put *them* in jail.

Mr. Morris, the guard who took me to see my dad, is taking me to my unit. I'm trying to keep up with him at the same time that I'm trying to check out everything around me. It really does look like a school except that there are some high fences and you have to have a key to go through almost every door.

"How come the guards don't have guns?" I ask Mr. Morris.

"Because we're not guards, we're staff. This ain't a jail."

We walk near a grassy area toward a brick building with *GH* on the front. Mr. Morris uses his key to open the glass doors.

"This is the day room," he says, showing me inside.

It's a wide-open area about the size of my aunt Macie's den. Along the back wall is a smaller room with a large glass window. Behind that, I see a tiled wall with showerheads sticking out.

Two black kids and three Hispanics, all dressed in gray sweat suits like me, are sitting at a long table like the one in my school cafeteria. Until a second ago they were watching the TV hanging near the ceiling. Now they're watching me.

"This is Graylin Alexander," Mr. Morris says to a black man who walks out of a glass enclosure. It seems like almost everybody who works here is either black or Mexican.

I peer behind him and see lots of buttons, computer screens and TV monitors.

"I'm Mr. Dennison," the man says, shaking my hand.

"He has a detention hearing on Tuesday." Mr. Morris rolls his eyes. "Another sexting case."

"I didn't sext *nobody*," I say. "I'm innocent."

Mr. Dennison nods as if he's heard this before. "Let's go over the rules."

I press my palms to my face. "I went over the rules already. Twice."

"And now we're going to do it one last time to make extra sure you don't forget."

I barely listen as he tells me the same rules all over again.

"You're in room number seven."

Looking down a long hallway, I see pairs of tennis shoes outside some of the rooms. "We can't wear shoes in our cells?"

"They ain't cells, they're rooms. And no, you can't wear shoes inside your room. Set them outside the door so the staff knows you're in there."

Mr. Dennison hands me a cloth bag containing deodorant and lotion.

"Dinner's at five. After dinner, once you get your homework done, you can watch TV until it's time to shower at seven-forty-five. Lights out at nine."

I wish he would hurry up because I'm tired.

"Wakeup time is six-fifteen," he continues. "You need to have your bed made and room cleaned by seven. School starts at eight-thirty. We all leave the building as a group. Everybody walks in lines of two. Did you understand everything I just said?"

"There's school on Saturday?"

Mr. Dennison smiles. "Sorry about that. No school tomorrow. And wake-up time is at seven on weekends. There's church on Sunday in the chapel if you want to go. Did you understand everything I said?"

"Yes, sir."

Mr. Dennison raises an eyebrow. "A kid with some manners. I like that."

"How many inmates are in here?"

"None. This ain't a prison. We have twelve rooms, but only eight other boys are here now." I follow him down the hallway. He opens a door with the number seven on it.

"This'll be your room for the next few days."

The room looks kind of like the prison cells on TV, except there aren't any bars or a toilet. My bedroom at home is about six times as big. There's a rectangular window on the door about the size of a sheet of paper. My eyes widen at the slab sticking out from the wall.

"I have to sleep on that hard cement without a mattress?"

Mr. Dennison laughs. "No, I'll get you a mattress."

"Do I get pajamas?"

"No pajamas. Sleep in your underwear."

"Do I have a cellmate?"

"No, you don't have a *roommate*. When the lights go out, the doors are locked from the outside."

My eyes get wide. My granny says never lock the doors from the outside. You can die in a fire like that. "But what if there's a fire? How do I get out?"

"We've never had a fire. Don't worry, we'll get you out if that happens."

"Can I keep the lights on?" I'm too embarrassed to tell him that I have a night light in my room at home.

He points up at the ceiling. "There's a dim light up there."

I look around. "Where's the light switch?"

"We control the lights from the booth up front. That one stays on all night so we can look into your room and check on you."

Mr. Dennison leaves and returns with a thin blanket and a worn, striped mattress about as thick as a double cheeseburger. I look up at him. "This is the mattress?"

"Yep. You'll be fine. You're just in time for dinner."

As soon as he says that, I realize that I haven't had anything to eat since breakfast and I'm suddenly starving. We go back into the day room where eight boys are now sitting around the table.

"We got a new kid on the block," one of them says as they all seem to approach me at once.

"What's your name?" somebody asks.

"Graylin."

A skinny, light-skinned black kid steps forward. "I'm Tyke. What you in for?"

I hesitate. "My attorney told me not to talk about my case."

"I don't care what your attorney told you. I asked you a question."

The other boys snicker. Tyke is obviously the bully of the group.

I stand a little taller and try to look tough. "I can't talk about my case."

"You think I'm a snitch or something? Cuz if that's what you trying to say about me, I'ma have to do something 'bout that."

My head starts to hurt. I don't need this bully bothering me on top of everything else I've been through today.

Before I can respond, Mr. Dennison walks up and Tyke changes his tune.

"Hey, Mr. Dennison, whazzup?"

Mr. Dennison ignores him as he removes plates from a metal container and hands one to each of us. We all sit down at the table to eat. I unwrap my plate to find chicken steak, tater tots, and broccoli. It tastes about the same as the food at school. My plate is empty in seconds.

I sense someone behind me and turn around to find Tyke hovering over me.

"Don't think I'm done with you," he whispers. "You can't call me a snitch and get away with it."

"I didn't call you a snitch."

"So now you callin' me a liar?"

I know it will only get worse if I let him know how scared I am. So I try to act hard. "Get outta my face."

The other boys start whooping with laughter, which makes Tyke's light skin darken like he's been sitting in the sun too long.

"You better not let me catch you alone," Tyke seethes. "Cuz if I do, I'ma mess you up."

# CHAPTER 14

## *Miguel*

I park my Volvo along the curb in front of the Carlyles' home in the View Park section of Los Angeles. The striking brick home is the length of two houses in my neighborhood.

As I'm about to get out of my car, a black BMW pulls into the driveway. A man climbs out and waits as I head up the brick-lined walkway.

"I'm Percy Carlyle, Kennedy's father. You must be from the District Attorney's Office. Thanks for coming by so early, and on a weekend, no less."

Mr. Carlyle is clean-shaven with angular features. He looks like a big-firm lawyer even in khakis and a Polo shirt.

I wait for him to pull out a key and open the door, but he knocks instead.

An attractive black woman answers and introduces herself as Simone Carlyle, Kennedy's mother. Her hair is pulled back in a tight bun and she's wearing dark jeans and a starched white shirt that's as stiff as the smile on her face. She acknowledges Percy Carlyle with something short of a nod.

The Carlyle's living room is the size of a two-car garage and is full of antique furniture with high backs and textured fabrics in deep red and burgundy. Heavy velvet curtains cover almost a complete wall, giving the room the feel of a funeral parlor. A teapot, tiny cookies, and expensive China sit in the middle of the coffee table. I wonder if it's intentional that the pink and yellow sprinkles on the cookies are the same color as the stripes along the rim of the teacups.

"I'd like you to know that the District Attorney's Office is taking this case very seriously," I begin. "We regret what happened to your daughter. I'll be prosecuting the case against the boy who was arrested. One of the things—"

"His name is Graylin Alexander, right?" Simone asks.

I hesitate. "How did you find out his name?"

"It's all over the school. That boy put my baby's picture on the Internet. Everybody needs to know his name."

I lean forward. "You have evidence that the picture is on the Internet?"

"No, she doesn't," Percy says, shooting Simone an annoyed side glance. "Go ahead. Finish what you were saying."

I tell them about the anonymous note and that the boy is charged with making a criminal threat as well as possession of child pornography.

"How many cases have you tried and how many guilty verdicts did you get?" Simone interrupts.

Percy rolls his eyes.

"I have a very solid record of success, Mrs. Carlyle," I say, trying to regain control of the conversation. "I'd really like to interview Kennedy. Is she here?"

Percy stands up. "I'll go get her."

Simone's eyes trail Percy out of the room. It's almost as if she's uncomfortable with him roaming the house unsupervised. I understand now why the man doesn't have a key. He probably doesn't want one.

Kennedy enters the living room holding her father's hand. She's a skinny girl with bangs and a long ponytail that extends past her shoulder blades. She looks dazed, as if she's just been roused from a deep sleep.

I introduce myself and begin with a few harmless questions about her classes and teachers to put her at ease.

"Do you have any idea how someone could've gotten a naked picture of you?" I ask after five minutes or so.

Kennedy lowers her head and answers in a shaky voice, "No."

"Do you know Graylin Alexander?"

She nods. "He's in two of my classes. But we're not friends or anything like that."

"Has he ever approached you or tried to talk to you?"

"No."

For the next twenty minutes or so, I ask a series of questions that yield nothing super helpful.

"Thanks for speaking with me. I'll need to talk to you again later on, but right now I'd like to speak with your parents."

"As you can see," Simone says once Kennedy is out of earshot, "this has been a very traumatic experience for my daughter. I don't know if she'll ever be the same."

I nod, hoping to appear empathetic. "I have a copy of the picture they found on the boy's phone. I'd like to see if you recognize the background. We need to determine where it was taken. I didn't want to show it to Kennedy yet, considering how fragile she appears to be."

"I don't want to see it." Percy gets to his feet and stalks out of the room.

"He's such a weak man," Simone hisses as she takes a sip of tea. "Let me see it."

I open a folder and hand Simone an 8x10 color photograph. "This is an enlargement, so it's a little blurry."

"Oh my God!" Simone presses her right hand to her chest. "That's Kennedy's room! That boy took that picture through my baby's bedroom window!"

# CHAPTER 15

## *Graylin*

I wake up to a loud voice and banging on my door.

"Time to get up! Time to get up!"

It takes me a few seconds to realize where I am. When I do, sadness swoops down on me like someone slapped a hood over my head.

Mr. Dennison is stomping down the hallway unlocking doors. "Time to get cleaned up and make up your bed. Be in the day room for breakfast in thirty minutes."

When I sit up, pain shoots across my back, probably from sleeping on that skinny mattress. The room feels as cold as the inside of a refrigerator.

I step outside my room and head into the day room. Two other boys are already in line for the bathroom.

"What you lookin' at?" Tyke appears from nowhere and is breathing down the back of my neck.

"I ain't forgot about you dissin' me."

I try my best to ignore him. When it's my turn, I wash my face and brush my teeth as fast as I can and go back to my room to make up my bed. When it's time to eat, we walk up to the cart and Mr. Dennison hands us trays with sausage, hash browns, orange juice and a fruit cup. I can feel Tyke watching me, but I refuse to look at him. I want to sit as far away from him as I can, but the day room isn't that big. A white kid with tattoos crawling up his pale neck calls out to me.

"Sit over here, homie."

The boy's greeting feels almost as good as a warm hug from my granny. He tells me his name is Andrew.

"What you in for?" he asks, even before I'm seated on the bench.

"For nothing," I mutter, happy to have someone nice to talk to. I'm about to say I can't talk about my case, but I don't want a repeat of the situation with Tyke.

"They said I sexted a naked picture of a girl at my school, but I didn't."

"Aw man!" His blue-green eyes almost start glowing. "You goin' down! My friend got a whole year at C-Y-A for that."

"What's C-Y-A?"

"California Youth Authority. Juvie prison."

I open my orange juice. "I'm not going nowhere. My dad hired me an attorney. Two attorneys. They're getting me out of here."

Andrew presses his fist to his mouth like it's a bullhorn and laughs. "I don't care how many attorneys you got. You crazy if you think you gettin' off."

I now regret sitting down next to Andrew and wish he would shut up.

"So you know your dad?" he asks.

I squint as if something's in my eye. "Of course I know my dad. He's coming to see me today."

"You rich or something?"

"No."

"I never met my dad," Andrew says with a shrug. "Don't nobody visit me."

Now I feel kind of sorry for him. "What about your mother or your granny? They don't come to see you?"

"Naw. I got a foster mother, but she can't get off work."

"Why are you in here?"

"Got into a fight with my foster brother and ran away. Broke his jaw." He puffs out his scrawny chest. "They charged me with assault and being a runaway."

He's smiling like he should get a prize or something. I want to tell him that's nothing to be proud of, but I don't.

"Stick with me," Andrew says. "I'll show you what's up. And don't worry about Tyke. He always messes with the new kids. Just ignore him."

Since it's Saturday, we get to go into the yard. As soon as we step outside, I hear my name being called. "Graylin, you've got a visitor."

When I see my dad coming up the walkway, I run over and hug him so tight we almost fall over.

"How you making out, Little Man?"

"I'm okay." I want to tell my dad about Tyke messing with me, but I figure he's already worried enough about me. I take him into my unit and Mr. Dennison lets me show him my room.

My dad looks all around, but doesn't say anything. We go back outside and sit on a bench by ourselves.

"When can I come home?" My voice gets shaky even though I'm trying hard not to cry.

"After your hearing on Tuesday. I'm sure that judge will see that you don't belong in here." My dad goes quiet for a long time, then stares at me real hard. "I need you to tell me what happened."

I wring my hands. "But Ms. Jenny and Ms. Angela said I wasn't supposed to talk about my case to nobody. Not even you."

"I don't care what they said!" My dad's nostrils get bigger. "Did you take a picture of that girl?"

I want to do what my attorneys said, but I can't disobey my dad. Anyway, I want him to know that I'm not guilty. "No."

"Then what was it doing on your phone?"

"Somebody sent it to me?"

"Who?"

"I don't know."

"What do you mean you don't know?"

"They sent it on Snapchat."

"What the hell is Snapchat?"

I try to explain how Snapchat works, but I can tell my dad isn't getting it.

"Well, if the picture disappears, why was it still on your phone?"

"Because I took a screenshot of it."

My dad brushes his hand down his face. "This is nuts. I don't see how they could punish you for having a picture when somebody else sent it to you. Everything's going to be okay." He pulls me so close he almost smothers me.

"My friend Andrew says his friend got sent to juvie prison for a year for sexting."

"Friend? These hoodlums in here ain't your friends! Didn't Ms. Jenny tell you not to talk to nobody about your case?"

"I didn't tell him anything."

"You better not. And don't be listening to these thugs. You ain't going to nobody's prison, you hear me?" My dad's voice is so angry he's scaring me. "That ain't gonna happen because I ain't gonna let it happen."

# CHAPTER 16

## *Angela*

I agree to meet Jenny at Woodcat, a trendy coffee shop on Sunset Boulevard in Echo Park. It's only twenty minutes away from Eastlake Juvenile Hall, where we'll be interviewing Graylin in an hour or so.

As soon as I walk in, I see Jenny seated at a table in the back.

"I was able to get a copy of the police report," she says, handing it to me before I can even sit down. "According to the report, Graylin did have a naked picture on his phone. I'll have to get the hows and whys from him."

It's a good sign that Jenny's willing to share the police report with me, but a bad one that she's still using the pronoun *I* rather than *we*. I was hoping she'd give my offer to help some consideration overnight and come to the realization that two heads are better than one.

I go to the counter to order coffee and an oatmeal cookie, then return to the table and start reading the police report.

"As I mentioned last night," Jenny begins, "it came as quite a surprise to me that you wanted to be part of Graylin's defense team."

*She certainly likes to cut to the chase.*

I turn the police report facedown. "Frankly, *I* didn't realize I wanted to participate until the words came out of my mouth. If you're worried about splitting the fee, that's a non-issue. I'm doing this *pro bono*."

"I'm sure you know this, but it's not a good idea to represent someone close to you. Emotion can interfere with legal judgment."

"That shouldn't be a problem in this case since I won't be the lead attorney." I try to stroke her ego a bit. "This is your case. I'll just be there to help you out."

I want and need to be part of Graylin's defense team. The charges he's facing are much too serious for me to sit on the sidelines. If Jenny doesn't want to share her sandbox, I'll have Gus fire her ass.

Jenny crosses her arms and leans back in her chair. "How much juvenile court experience have you had?"

"Not much. Primarily representing child trafficking victims on solicitation charges. But I was an assistant U.S. Attorney before going out on my own. I know my way around a courtroom. Why are you so opposed to having me help out?"

"Representing a kid is very different from representing an adult client. Children are very emotional, their parents too. You're part attorney and part therapist. You also have to manage expectations, which you didn't do last night."

"Excuse me?"

"You told Gus that Graylin would get to go home when you had no idea whether that was the case."

"I was just trying to keep him upbeat. How about this?" It feels like I'm groveling and I hate myself for it. "The minute something happens that makes you feel this isn't working out, say the word and I'll bow out."

Several tense seconds pass, then Jenny's thin lips flatten into a taut smile. "Okay, I guess. For now."

I figure that's the best I'm going to get. So I let it go and make an effort to get to know her. "How did you end up doing juvenile defense?"

"I thought I was going to change the world." She laughs. "My older brother got arrested for possession of forty bucks worth of marijuana when he was sixteen. He ended up with a prosecutor who threw the book at him and a public defender who was too overworked to give his case any real attention. He spent a year at a juvenile camp and was never the same after that. He's been in and out of prison most of his life. I went to law school because I was on a mission to keep that from happening to other kids."

"Sounds like you're doing it."

"Not the way I'd hoped. The juvenile system is just as over-burdened as the adult side. And all this energy the D.A.'s Office is putting into crucifying kids for sexting is nuts."

"Is sexting really a big problem?"

Instead of answering, Jenny pulls her iPad from her purse, taps the screen a few times, then hands it to me. "Take a look at that."

The screen shows the Los Angeles Unified School District's website. Several pages are dedicated to warning students and parents about sexting. They even have an official campaign, *Now Matters Later*, to educate students about using social media responsibly.

I had no idea teen sexting was so prevalent. "With all the serious crimes in the world, I just don't understand why prose-cutors are going after kids."

"Because they can," Jenny says. "Also the law hasn't caught up with technology. Some states recognize that. In New York, a kid caught with a picture of a naked minor on his phone would have to participate in a counseling program warning him about the legal consequences of sexting. California and most other states haven't gotten on board yet."

All I can do is shake my head.

"I blame prosecutors," Jenny continues. "As far as I'm concerned, they're abusing their discretion. Some of them will treat the immature fifteen-year-old who sends a picture of his penis to his girlfriend as harshly as the malicious bully who forces a classmate to strip and posts her picture all over Instagram."

Jenny stops to take a sip of coffee. "And in the process, they're needlessly destroying a whole lot of young lives."

# CHAPTER 17

## *Angela*

When we arrive at juvenile hall, Graylin hugs us like we're his long-lost sisters.

"My dad was here," he says, beaming. "But they only let him stay for three hours. Tomorrow he can stay for four hours because it's Sunday."

Visiting hours for parents are limited to weekends and following court appearances, but there are no restrictions on lawyer visits.

"Have you talked to anybody about your case since we spoke yesterday?" Jenny asks.

Graylin looks down at the floor. "Um, well, not really."

"What do you mean *not really*?"

"Um, my new friend Andrew asked me what I was in for. I had to say something because he was being friendly. So I just said I was accused of sexting and that was it. I swear."

"What about your dad? Did you talk to him about your case?"

"I told him you said I wasn't supposed to, but he made me. He only wanted to know whether I took the picture and I told him I didn't. Please don't tell him I told you. He'll be mad at me."

Jenny pins a stern look on Graylin. "Going forward, it's important that you don't talk to *anybody* else about your case. Okay?"

Graylin nods. "Okay. I won't."

She pulls a pamphlet from her satchel and hands it to Graylin. "I want you to read this. It explains how the juvenile court process works."

She hands another copy to me. "You should read it too."

I glance at the title and stiffen. *Understanding the Juvenile Delinquency System.* Is she trying to belittle me in front of *our* client?

"Why does Ms. Angela need one?" Graylin asks. "Doesn't she know this stuff?"

"Of course I do," I reply with a phony smile. "I'm going to give my copy to your father."

Jenny takes out a yellow legal pad. "I want you to tell me everything you can remember about what happened on Friday. The police report says you had a naked picture of a girl from your school on your phone. Is that true?"

Graylin blows out a breath.

"It's okay to talk to us," I prod him. "Whatever you tell us is protected by the attorney-client privilege."

Graylin squints. "What does that mean?"

Jenny hurls a chiding look my way and I instantly realize my mistake. I'm talking to Graylin as if he were an adult, not a kid.

"That means whatever you tell me, even if it's something you did that's bad," Jenny explains, "I have to keep it a secret. I can't tell *anybody* about it unless you give me permission."

"And Ms. Angela too? She can't tell anybody either, right?"

I nod. "That's correct."

"Not even my dad or my granny or my Uncle Dre?"

"Not even them," Jenny confirms. "That's one of the rules attorneys have to follow."

He doesn't look at us. "Um, yeah. I had the naked picture of Kennedy on my phone."

"Did you take it?" Jenny asks.

"No, ma'am." Graylin raises his right hand. "I swear on the Bible."

"Then how did it get on your phone?"

"Somebody sent it to me on Snapchat."

"But Snapchat pictures disappear," I say.

"As soon as I saw it, I took a screenshot of it."

"Do you know who sent it to you?" Jenny asks.

Graylin shakes his head.

Jenny frowns. "You have to click on the sender's name to open the picture, don't you?"

"Yeah. But I didn't know them."

Jenny scribbles something down on her legal pad. "Do you remember the name?"

"It wasn't a name. Just some letters and a number. I don't remember what they were."

"When did you first see it?"

"Right before first period ended."

"Describe the picture," I say. "Could you tell where it was taken?"

Jenny stretches her palm out toward me, her eyes still on Graylin. "Let's slow down. It's best if we ask him one question at a time. Describe the picture for us, Graylin."

My jaw tightens from her rebuke. I keep my mouth shut and let the prima donna do her thing.

"It looked like she was in somebody's house and she didn't have any clothes on."

"What part of the house?" Jenny asks.

"A bedroom, I think."

"Was she posing for the picture? Like a selfie?"

"No. It looked like it was taken through a window because it was kinda far away."

"And you have no idea who sent it to you?"

"No, ma'am."

Jenny takes Graylin through every second of his day on Friday, starting with his arrival at school, his discovery of the Snapchat message and ending with his arrest.

"Ms. Jenny, how did the principal know I had the picture?"

"Someone left an anonymous note in the administration office saying you had a naked picture of Kennedy on your phone and that you were going to beat her up and post her picture all over Instagram."

Graylin rockets to his feet. "That's a lie! Somebody's lying on me!"

"We know Graylin." I rub his arm and guide him back to his seat. "And we're going to prove it."

"Did you have any other pictures of Kennedy on your phone?" Jenny asks.

"No, ma'am."

Jenny scans the questions on her legal pad. "Did you send the picture to anyone?"

"Nope. Nobody."

"Did you show it to anyone?"

"No, ma'am."

"Did you tell anyone about it?"

Graylin pauses for the first time and averts his eyes. "No, ma'am."

"We need you to be honest with us," Jenny reminds him again. "If you tell us something that isn't true, it might hurt your case because we won't be prepared."

He starts rubbing his palms up and down his thighs. "I was going to show it to my friend Crayvon, but I didn't get the chance."

"What's Crayvon's last name?"

"Little. I saw him when we were leaving first period. I told him I had something I wanted to show him. But I didn't get the chance."

"Why not?"

"He had to go to the administration office to—"

Light fills his eyes and Graylin springs to his feet again. "Crayvon must've been the one who sent me the picture and left that note! He's supposed to be my friend. Why would he do that to me?" He starts to cry.

"Hold on Graylin," Jenny says. "You said you didn't get a chance to tell Crayvon about it. How would he know you even had it?"

"Because he must've sent it to me! He left that note in the office and set me up!"

I stand up and hug him. "We don't know that for sure, but we'll look into it."

It takes us several minutes to calm Graylin down.

It's clear that Jenny is much more skilled at retrieving information from child clients than I am. I want to know more about Crayvon Little. But since that subject upset Graylin so much, she moves on to another topic.

"Let's go over how the police got your phone again."

Graylin hangs his head in an exaggerated show of exhaustion. "We went over that already. I'm getting tired, Ms. Jenny."

"I know. We'll take a break in a minute."

He exhales. "At first, when they asked me for it, I said it was in my locker. But then it started ringing."

"And then what happened?

"The Asian cop made me take it out of my pocket and give it to them, so I did."

Both of us jerk to attention at the same time. The first time Graylin recounted what happened, he made it sound as if he willingly handed over his phone.

"What do you mean he *made* you give it to him?" Jenny asks.

"The Asian cop was really mean. He said, *Give me the damn phone* and pounded the table with his fist."

Jenny and I gaze at each other with lawyerly glee.

"Did they read you your rights before they started talking to you?"

"Nope. I kept telling them that my dad told me not to talk to the police without his permission, but they wouldn't stop asking me questions. So can you get me out because they didn't read me my rights?"

"We'll see," Jenny says.

"Let's take a break." She motions me toward the door. "We'll be right back."

Once we're outside in the hallway, Jenny bites her lip and starts pacing. "The biggest problem we have is that Graylin saved the picture to his phone. That makes the possession charge hard for us to kick."

*Progress!* She's finally using the pronouns *we* and *us* as if we're a team.

"Sounds like our best shot is filing a motion to suppress the picture and Graylin's statements because the police violated his Fourth and Fifth Amendment rights."

"That's not our best shot," Jenny says. "It's our only shot."

# CHAPTER 18

## *Kennedy*

I hate it *so* much when my parents argue.

I crack my bedroom door and take a few steps into the hallway so I can see into the living room. My parents are standing nose-to-nose.

"This is a decision *both* of us have to make," my dad says.

"I understand that," my mom spits at him. "What I don't understand is why you want to sweep everything under the rug."

"I just don't think it's a good idea to make our daughter the poster child for sexting. You had no right to call the mayor's office throwing around *my* name without *my* permission."

"We've raised a ton of money for that man. He owes us."

"Don't you understand that pushing this case means the media could pick up on it? That could cause even more embarrassment for her."

"There's nothing for Kennedy to be embarrassed about. Some pervert took a picture of her through her bedroom window. I want to teach my daughter to stand up for herself."

My dad throws up his hands and slumps to the couch.

I don't understand how my mom and dad started hating each other. Last Christmas, everyone was so happy. Then out of the blue, my dad sat me down and told me he was moving out.

"And why won't you go to counseling with us?" my mom asks. "Lord knows everybody in this house could use it."

He stands up, his hands at his waist. "I'm fine with Kennedy getting counseling, but I have no desire to air our dirty laundry before some stranger. So don't ask me again."

They're both quiet now, staring at each other like two frozen statues. I don't want to be like other kids at my school who have to go back and forth between their divorced parents like ping-pong balls.

"There's something I need to tell you," my dad says. "Please have a seat." He pats the space on the couch next to him.

"Oh, so you're finally going to admit that you're having an affair."

"I'm not having an affair! For Christ's sake! Will you please sit down?"

My mom takes the armchair across from him.

"The governor is about to appoint me to the Superior Court bench. They're going to be examining every area of my life. It won't look good if my daughter is embroiled in the middle of a sexting scandal."

My mom's mouth gapes open, but no words come out.

"So can you do me this one favor? Just let the D.A.'s Office handle this without our active involvement?"

When she's super mad, my mom doesn't raise her voice. Her next words are extra soft. "Sounds like the only thing you're concerned about is your career." She leans back in the chair and crosses her legs.

My dad doesn't say anything and lets my mom keep talking.

"I couldn't care less about you being appointed to the bench. As soon as you're confirmed you're probably going to run off with some little slut. We might as well just end this charade now. I'm contacting a divorce attorney tomorrow. I'm done."

"C'mon, Simone, can't we—"

"And for the record, in addition to taking you to the cleaners, I'm going to make sure that boy gets put in jail for as long as they'll have him."

She stands up. "I'd appreciate it if you'd leave."

My dad slowly gets to his feet.

I go back into my room, tears streaming down my face. As I sink onto my bed, my phone chirps. I pick it up and read the text from my best friend LaShay. When I hear screaming, I don't even realize that it's me.

My parents rush into the room, nearly tripping over each other in the doorway. My mom throws her arms around me. "What's the matter, baby?"

I can't speak, so I hand her my phone.

"Oh my God!" she shrieks after reading the text, then shoves the phone into my dad's face.

When my dad reads it, he looks like he wants to scream too.

"Now are you ready to fight for your daughter?" my mom yells at him. "Or is everything still all about you?"

# CHAPTER 19

## *Angela*

Jenny and I spend most of Monday morning at her Echo Park office preparing for Graylin's arraignment and detention hearing.

We interview Graylin's minister and two of his teachers by phone and review every report card and award Gus could find. We scour Graylin's Snapchat, Instagram, Facebook, Twitter and Tumblr accounts, as well as his laptop and emails.

"When do you think we're going to get a look at the picture and Graylin's phone?" I ask.

"The fact that the D.A. assigned to the case hasn't returned my calls isn't a good sign. I put a few feelers out and they came back mixed. Miguel Martinez hates putting away kids for sexting, but he thinks juvenile court is beneath him."

We start gathering up our papers and thirty minutes later we're back at juvenile hall sitting with Graylin. Gus is on speakerphone.

"We want to explain what's going to happen in court tomorrow," Jenny begins, looking Graylin in the eyes. "It's going to be like a mini-trial. Even though there won't be a jury, you need to understand that the judge is the jury. So sit up straight, don't make any faces and respond clearly when the judge asks you a question."

Graylin begins to fidget, thumping his fingers on the desk. "What are they going to ask me?"

"The judge is going to read the charges against you and ask if you understand them." Jenny pulls out a piece of paper. "The first charge is possession of child pornography. Do you know what that means?"

"Um, yeah. Child pornography is having naked pictures, right?"

"Yes, of someone under the age of eighteen. The judge is going to ask whether you admit or deny the petition? You need to respond *deny*. I'll give you a signal when it's time to say that."

"Is deny the same thing as not guilty?"

"Exactly. And the second charge is making a criminal threat. You're going to say *deny* to both."

"Can I tell the judge that I didn't write that note and that Crayvon set me up?"

"No," Jenny says. "We're still looking into that."

"What's Crayvon got to do with this?" Gus' voice booms through the phone.

"Nothing that we're sure of yet," I say.

"Ms. Jenny, if they're charging me with having a naked picture on my phone, how do I get off since I *did* have a naked picture?"

Graylin is indeed a smart kid.

"You leave that to me. The only issue the court is going to deal with tomorrow is whether your home is a suitable place for you to be while your case is pending."

Jenny expresses surprise that the Probation Department hasn't contacted Gus yet and tells him to expect a call sometime today. "They're going to ask you a bunch of questions about Graylin's home life. You must show that he'll be under twenty-four-hour supervision."

"My mother will be home with him while I'm at work. My sister's going to help homeschool him."

"I can't go back to school?" Graylin says, crestfallen.

"No, not until your case is resolved."

He folds his arms and slides down in his chair.

Jenny points a finger at him. "You can't do that in court tomorrow. Please sit up. If something happens that you don't like, you have to ignore it. I know this is hard on you, but I need you to follow my instructions, okay?"

"Yeah, okay."

"C'mon, Little Man," Gus says. "Everything's gonna be fine. You gotta do what your attorneys say."

"Is Kennedy going to be there?" Graylin asks.

"I doubt it. I've never had a victim show up at a detention hearing, but you never know."

"I wouldn't worry about it," I say. "You'll get to go home tomorrow."

Jenny purses her lips and rolls her eyes. I did it again. Telling Graylin something I don't know for sure. I'll apologize to Jenny later.

We spend the next hour taking Gus and Graylin through mock questioning. After Jenny lobs all the softball questions, I play the role of the prosecutor and take them through the wringer.

One of the staff arrives to escort Graylin back to his unit and Jenny and I head for our cars, which are parked behind each other on Eastlake Avenue.

Jenny gets into her car, then abruptly jumps out and marches up to me.

"Please don't do that again." Her lips are twisted up like a pretzel.

"Do what again?"

"You told Graylin everything's going to be fine and that he's going home tomorrow. You can't keep saying stuff just to make him feel good."

"I'm sorry. It kind of slipped out. But based on the facts, Graylin should—"

"That's the operative word, *should*. Child clients take you at your word and when you can't deliver, it destroys their trust. If you want to stay on this defense team, then stop undercutting me."

Before I can respond, Jenny struts back to her car and screeches off.

# Chapter 20

## *Graylin*

It's dinnertime, but I'm not hungry. I stare at my hamburger and wish I was home. I miss my granny's cooking, especially her fried chicken.

"You too good to eat, Smart Boy?"

Tyke is sitting down across from me. I don't look up.

"I'm talkin' to you, Smart Boy."

Tyke needs to leave me alone. I have a headache and my stomach hurts because I'm nervous about going to court tomorrow.

"Well, I ain't talking to you, Dumb Boy."

"Whoa!" all the other boys exclaim at once.

I've just embarrassed Tyke, but I don't care. I have too many other problems to worry about. Besides, Tyke can't do anything to me with Mr. Dennison so close by.

"Dude, do you know who I am?" Tyke's face twists with rage.

"I'm not messing with you. So don't mess with me."

I take a bite of my hamburger just as Tyke hurls his milk carton across the table. The corner of the carton hits me below my right eye. The whole right side of my face goes numb. When I press my hand to my cheek and see a spot of blood on my finger, I explode.

Diving across the table, I start pounding Tyke in the face with a force I didn't know I had.

Mr. Dennison snatches me by my sweatshirt and pulls me away while another man grabs Tyke. I break free and jump on top of Tyke. I'm sitting on his chest now, pounding him in the face with both fists. He screams like a girl and tries to cover his face.

It takes Mr. Dennison *and* Mr. Morris to pull me off of him. I'm still crying and swinging at the air as they drag me to the opposite side of the day room.

"I didn't even do anything to him and he threw his milk at me and tried to put my eye out!" I sob.

"I didn't do nothin' to him," Tyke yells from the floor. "He just jumped up and started punchin' me. I swear!"

"Don't matter who threw the first punch," Mr. Dennison barks. "Both of you are in big trouble!"

# CHAPTER 21

## *Angela*

Jenny is already at the courthouse when I arrive the next morning. We haven't spoken since her little hissy fit yesterday. She greets me with such a gigantic smile I'm beginning to think she might be bipolar.

"You look awful happy," I say as I step into the attorney meeting room.

"That's because I just finished reading this." Jenny waves a document in the air. "The detention report recommends that Graylin go home!" She hands it to me. "Graylin should be here any minute."

I'm happy to hear that news, but I have something else on my mind. The negative residue from our tiff needs to be addressed.

"Hey, Jenny," I begin, "I wanted to say that I'm sorry about—"

She flashes me her palm. "Just don't let it happen again."

I don't like her dismissiveness and I'm about to tell her as much when the door opens and a sheriff's deputy shows Graylin into the room.

"Oh my God!" I run over and cup Graylin's face. "What happened to you?" His right eye is almost swollen shut and there's a long, red gash underneath it.

"This boy named Tyke threw a carton of milk at me. But I got him good. He won't be messing with me again."

The door opens and Gus walks in. When his eyes land on Graylin, he cringes. "What in the hell happened to your face?"

Graylin hurls his arms around his dad. "This bully started messing with me for nothing."

"This is not good," Jenny says. "The detention report recommends sending you home. But it was obviously completed before the fight. This could change things."

"That's not fair!" Graylin whines. "Tyke was the one messing with me. I was only defending myself."

"The fact that somebody nearly put my son's eye out shows we need to get him the hell out of here for his own safety."

"I need you to step outside," Jenny says to Gus. "We need to find out what happened so we're not hit with any surprises."

"He just needs to tell the truth," Gus says. "He—"

"I need you to step outside," Jenny says firmly.

Gus sulks out like an angry child.

Jenny fires off a ton of questions at Graylin while furiously taking notes. Five minutes later, a deputy knocks on the door to tell us his case is being called.

Juvenile court operates in a more casual atmosphere than adult court. In this one, the judge sits on an elevated bench, next to the witness box. There's no jury box and the court reporter sits below the bench facing the judge.

The three of us take seats at the defense table with Graylin in the middle. Gus and Dre are on the back row, along the wall. A well-dressed black couple is seated on the opposite side of the courtroom. Since juvenile proceedings are closed to the public, I assume they must be the girl's parents.

When a GQ-looking Hispanic man carrying a stack of folders walks in, Jenny rises and approaches him.

"I'm Jenny Ungerman, Graylin Alexander's attorney. I left a couple of messages for you. Any idea when we can get a copy of the picture and the note? We'd also like to examine Graylin's phone."

"Oh, yeah, sorry. Crazy schedule," Miguel Martinez says. "I should have the picture and note to you by the end of the week. I'll need more time with the phone. We sent it to an outside firm to take a look at it."

He's about to sit down when he notices Graylin's swollen face. His expression tells me it's as much of a surprise to him as it was to us.

"I'm concerned that they're doing outside analysis on the phone," Jenny says, when she sits back down. "The D.A.'s Office doesn't spend that kind of money on a case like this. Something's up."

The bailiff calls the courtroom to order and everyone stands as Judge Jaynie Miller enters from a side door and takes the bench. "Good morning, everyone!"

I've never seen a judge walk into court with such a cheerful disposition. The judge looks so happy I almost expect her to start waving like she's on a parade float. Her short brown hair is lightly sprinkled with blonde highlights and her cheeks are a soft rosy color.

Judge Miller examines the paperwork in front of her. "Looks like we're here for an arraignment and detention hearing." She rattles off the charges. "Does the minor—" Graylin's puffy face stops her mid-sentence. "Does the minor admit or deny the petition?"

In juvenile court, minors typically are not referred to by their name on the record.

Jenny gently elbows Graylin.

"I deny," he says loudly.

"I've read the detention report. Mr. Martinez, do you wish to be heard?"

"Yes, Your Honor. We feel strongly that the minor should be detained. The victim's parents—who are here in court today—fear that the minor presents a very real threat to their daughter. Simone Carlyle, the victim's mother, would like to be heard regarding the trauma her daughter has suffered. In addition, Mrs. Carlyle recently advised me that the picture has gone viral."

I place a gentle hand on Graylin's shoulder. I can feel him shaking.

Jenny scribbles something on a Post-it note, folds it and passes it to me behind Graylin's back.

I cringe when I read it. *Viral=Problem!*

"Okay," Judge Miller says. "I'll briefly hear from the mother."

Mrs. Carlyle rises and absently tinkers with her pearl necklace. "I want the court to know that my baby is very distraught and embarrassed over this massive invasion of her privacy. Both physically and psychologically she's a wreck. She cries every day, all day."

The woman stops to dab at the corner of her eye with a tissue. "And ever since my baby's friend texted her with the news that the picture has gone viral, she's been afraid to leave the house. It's probably in the hands of pedophiles now. My husband and I are here today to beg the court to keep that boy locked up so my child is safe."

"But I didn't do nothing, Ms. Angela," Graylin mutters.

"Please be quiet," I whisper.

The judge directs a question to Martinez. "Any prior contact between the minor and the victim?"

"Nothing beyond attending the same school and having a couple of classes together."

The judge turns to Jenny. "Any questions for Mrs. Carlyle?"

"Just one," Jenny says.

"Mrs. Carlyle, has your daughter seen a counselor as a result of this incident?"

Simone's chin juts forward. "No, not yet."

"No further questions, Your Honor."

Jenny's done with her, but Mrs. Carlyle keeps talking.

"You're trying to make it seem like my daughter wasn't damaged by that little pervert!"

"Mrs. Carlyle," the judge says, "there isn't a question pending."

"Your Honor," Jenny exclaims, "I object to—"

"But I didn't do nothing," Graylin cries out. "I'm innocent. I swear!"

The judge gently taps her gavel. "Young man, you are not allowed to speak unless a question is directed to you."

A tear falls from Graylin's swollen eye and in seconds, his hiccupping sobs fill the courtroom.

"Your Honor," Jenny says. "Can we take a short break to give my client a chance to collect himself?"

Judge Miller twists her lips to the side. "Let's take fifteen."

# CHAPTER 22

## Dre

My buddy Gus is close to a meltdown.

"That girl's parents act like Graylin killed somebody!"

He's sitting next to me with his head in his hands. We're the only ones in the courtroom now besides the clerk and the bailiff. Angela and Jenny took Graylin outside to calm him down.

"Just keep it together, man. It's gonna be okay."

"Graylin's a good kid. I don't understand why they came at him like that."

I nudge his arm. "Let's step outside and get some air."

Without responding, Gus follows me out of the courtroom. We maneuver down a wide hallway packed with kids and parents.

I'm exiting the courthouse doors before I realize that Gus isn't behind me. I rush back inside, but it takes forever for the sheriff's deputy to wave me through the metal detectors.

As I scan the lobby, alarm sets in. Gus is walking toward a corner of the building where the girl's parents are standing. I make it over there just as Gus reaches them.

"I'm Graylin's father," Gus says, directing his attention to the man. "I wonder if I could speak to you for a minute. My son is a good kid. He—"

His wife gets in Gus' face. "Your son is a predator and a pervert who belongs behind bars."

Gus recoils like he's just been slapped. It takes a couple of seconds for him to respond.

"Ma'am, I know what they charged him with, but he's innocent. His life shouldn't be ruined because someone sent him that picture."

"You apparently don't know your child. If I have anything to say about it, he's going away for a long, long time. And when the criminal case is over, I'm suing you for emotional distress."

I've never seen Gus speechless, but I *have* seen him on the verge of exploding, and he's almost there. I step in and turn to the father. "I'm Dre, a family friend. We're sorry about what happened to your daughter. But the police have this all wrong."

The man runs a hand down his face. I can tell he doesn't wear the pants in his house.

"I agree with you," he says. "I don't think this situation warrants the death penalty either and I'm shocked at how it's being handled."

His wife looks as if she's about to swallow her tongue. "Percy! Have you lost your mind? You're going to stand right here in front of me and undercut your own daughter?"

Her voice is so loud one of the sheriff's deputies begins stalking toward us. "Is everything okay over here?"

"No, it isn't," the woman snaps. "This man threatened us. He's trying to force us to drop the charges against his son."

Gus' eyes widen. "What? I didn't—"

"This will have to be reported to the judge." The deputy takes out a small notepad from his shirt pocket. "Ma'am, what's your name?"

"Simone Carlyle."

"I'll also need the name of your judge?"

"No, you won't." The words from the girl's father surprise everyone. "This man didn't threaten anybody. My wife's overreacting."

The woman sneers at her husband with such disgust that the sheriff's deputy takes a step back.

"You need to make your case to the judge or the prosecutor, not us," the man says to Gus. "This is out of our hands."

He takes his wife by the forearm, but she jerks away and struts off down the hallway.

Angela and Jenny rush over. "What happened?" Angela asks.

"I just wanted to talk to them," Gus says, rubbing his chin. "To tell them Graylin was a good kid. But that witch lied and told the sheriff I was threatening them."

Jenny presses three fingers to her temples. "If they report this to the judge, the only person who's going to suffer is Graylin."

"But she's lying. Her husband even backed me up."

"Doesn't matter," Jenny says, turning to Angela. "Call Graylin's minister and teacher. They should've been here by now. We're definitely going to need their testimony."

# CHAPTER 23

## Angela

"I understand from one of the deputies that there was some kind of commotion between the parents during the break," Judge Miller says, once we're back in the courtroom. "Is there anything we need to discuss?"

Martinez stands and to my surprise says, "No, Your Honor."

There's a gasp from Mrs. Carlyle, who springs up from her seat, shoots a dirty look at Martinez, then sashays her way out of the courtroom. Her husband shakes his head.

I'm relieved, but not for long. Martinez calls one of the Eastlake staff to testify about Graylin's fight. The detention services officer tells the judge that after he separated the fighting boys, Graylin was so enraged that he charged at the other kid a second time, pounding him in the face while he lay on the floor. The boy ended up with a broken jaw.

On cross, Jenny establishes that the kid has bullied other boys at Eastlake and that Graylin didn't start the fight.

After putting the police report into evidence, Martinez has no additional witnesses and hands the floor to Jenny. She expertly rolls through a short examination of Graylin's science teacher, then his minister. They credibly testify that Graylin is a smart, responsible young man who is always respectful. They tell the judge that he's never been in any trouble and that Gus is a great father who's always on hand for parent-teacher meetings and who attends church regularly with his son.

On cross, Martinez makes a half-hearted attempt to get the teacher to say something negative about Graylin, but fails. He passes on even trying to cross the minister.

It's close to noon by the time Gus takes the stand. His hands are trembling and he continuously cracks his knuckles.

"What do you do for a living, Mr. Alexander?" Jenny begins.

"I rehab houses?"

"How long have you done that?"

"Two years?"

"And what did you do before that?"

Gus pauses.

We thoroughly prepped him for this question. It's always best to get negative information out on direct so you can control how it's presented.

"I was in prison for three years. For possession of cocaine."

"Were you dealing cocaine?"

"No. Just a user. Had a bad habit, but I kicked it. Been clean for five years."

"Are you close to your son?"

"Yes. Very close. His mother," he pauses again. "His mother's a crack addict. We don't know where she is. I'm raising my son with my mother's and sister's help. He's a good kid. An A student. Never gives me any trouble. Very mannerable. Always says *yes, sir* and *no, sir*. His grandmother, my moms, makes sure of that."

Gus is relaxed and almost smiling.

"If your son is released, who would supervise him?"

"I would be there in the mornings and after work. During the day my mother or my sister Macie would be at the house with him. He'll be homeschooled for now."

"What about his schoolwork? How would he get that done?"

"He's very self-motivated. I've never had to push him to do his homework. He likes school."

The second Jenny turns Gus over to Martinez, he stiffens like a slab of granite.

"Mr. Alexander, were you ever in any fights when you were in Corcoran State Prison?"

Jenny is on her feet before I can even process the question.

"Objection, Your Honor. That's irrelevant to this proceeding."

"Your Honor, the custodial parent's propensity for violence is quite relevant to whether the minor's home is a fit place for him."

"Mr. Alexander hasn't been in any trouble since his release three years ago," Jenny counters.

Judge Miller seems to wobble. "I'd like to hear it. Go ahead, Mr. Alexander."

Anger edges Gus' face. "I was in one fight."

"You broke another inmate's nose, correct?"

"I was defending myself from an attack. Prison isn't a great place. Neither is juvenile hall."

I inhale. Gus needs to answer the questions without the added commentary. If Martinez sees that he can get him angry, he'll keep pushing his buttons until he does.

"When you were out doing drugs, who was home with your then nine or ten-year-old son?"

"My mother or my sister."

"Were there times when the minor was left home alone while you were off someplace smoking crack?"

"Objection," Jenny says. "What happened three years ago isn't relevant to my client's current home life."

"I'll hear it," Judge Miller says.

Gus' lips press together as if he's trying to prevent something from escaping. "I was a different person back then. I don't understand why you're trying to make my son out to be a criminal? He's just a kid. A damn near perfect kid."

The judge peers over at Gus. "Just answer the question, Mr. Alexander. And please watch your language."

Gus' knuckles protrude as he grips the arms of the chair. "Yes, ma'am, sorry. Yeah, there were probably a couple of times when he was home alone, but nothing happened. That's all in the past. I've been a model citizen since I got out of prison."

"Is it true that your best friend," Martinez looks down at his notes, "Andre Thomas is a convicted drug dealer?"

"Yes," Gus says tightly. "And he's turned his life around too."

"And Mr. Thomas—a convicted drug dealer—spends time with your son too, correct? He's even here in court today." Martinez gazes toward Dre at the back of the courtroom. So does the judge.

Martinez's questions are pissing me off. So I know Gus is having an even harder time.

He bites his lower lip. "Yeah. He's a good dude."

"Do you drink alcohol, Mr. Alexander?"

Gus squints. "I'm a social drinker. Nothing excessive."

"What about weed? Do you smoke weed, Mr. Alexander?"

"Um…" Gus looks at Jenny as if he needs some signal telling him whether he should answer honestly. "Not really."

"Not really? Your son told his intake officer that you do indeed smoke weed."

Graylin lowers his head and starts wringing his hands.

"Weed is legal now," Gus says. "Yeah, I smoke occasionally, but never in front of my son."

"Then how would your son know you smoked weed if you didn't do it in front of him?"

"I don't know. Maybe he smelled it on me."

Martinez seems to be waiting for an explosion that doesn't come. I'm proud of Gus for keeping his cool.

"What's your monthly income, Mr. Alexander?"

"It depends on how many houses we flip. And sometimes I do tile work for a couple of real estate agents. But on average, not including flipping a house, I make about six hundred a week."

"How are you able to send your son to an expensive private school like Marcus Preparatory Academy if you only make six hundred dollars a week?"

Gus looks up at Martinez with furious, hooded eyes. "He also has a scholarship and my sister helps out when I'm running short."

"Are you certain your son's tuition money comes from flipping houses and not from selling drugs?"

"Objection!" Jenny yells. Her cheeks are flaming red. "There's no foundation for that question!"

Before the judge can rule on the objection, Gus loses it.

"Damn, this! This is some bull!"

The judge taps her gavel. "Mr. Alexander, I've warned you once. You will not use that kind of disrespectful language in my courtroom. Your inability to control your temper is clearly a reflection of the kind of home your son would be released to. And I'll tell you right now, I'm having my reservations."

I see tears begin to puddle in Gus' eyes.

"This ain't right. Y'all trying to railroad my son. He didn't do nothing to deserve this. God knows this ain't right!"

The judge bangs her gavel so hard, I think it might crack. "One more outburst from you, Mr. Alexander, and you'll be back behind bars for contempt of court."

# CHAPTER 24

## *Angela*

Judge Miller dismisses us for lunch following Gus' testimony. It's after one o'clock when we reconvene. She wastes no time announcing her decision.

"The purpose of a detention hearing is to determine whether it's in the best interest of the minor to remain in custody or return home. To keep a minor detained, there must be evidence that being in the parent's custody is contrary to the child's welfare."

I glance over at Graylin. He's squinting and leaning forward as if he can't quite hear.

"I'm impressed with this young man on many fronts. He's an excellent student, and based on the testimony of his teacher and minister, he's smart, responsible, and motivated. So Mr. Alexander, I applaud you for the great job you've done raising your son as a single parent."

I begin to relax. The judge is going to do the right thing and send Graylin home.

"However, there are three issues that concern me. First, this isn't the typical sexting case. The picture of the victim—which has now gone viral—was taken through the bedroom window of her home, an incredible invasion of her privacy. As you know,

I must consider the allegations before me to be true. Because the minor is so young, I fear this could be the start of other, more serious and violent behavior."

Graylin turns to look at me, his face a kaleidoscope of confusion. "But I didn't take that picture, Ms. Angela," he whispers. "I swear I didn't."

I squeeze his forearm and continue focusing on the judge.

"I'm also required to consider the victim's wishes in reaching my decision. This has been a very traumatic experience for her, as indicated by her mother's testimony. Mrs. Carlyle honestly fears for her daughter's safety if the minor is released.

"Finally, the fact that the minor was involved in a fight while in custody shows that he has violent tendencies. I also have concerns about the father's ability to supervise the child, due to his use of alcohol and marijuana, his close relationship with a convicted drug dealer, his own criminal past and his obvious inability to control his temper."

I lower my head and close my eyes.

"For these reasons, I don't believe it's in the best interest of the minor to return home. Therefore, I'm ordering that the minor be detained until final adjudication."

"Your Honor," Jenny says, standing up. "May I be heard?"

"You may, but it's not going to change my mind."

"My client has never been in trouble before and makes excellent grades. He has always thrived in his home environment and we think he will continue to do so if released. Would you consider house arrest?"

"I've made my decision, counselor." She bangs her gavel, rises and disappears through a door behind the bench.

On the back row, Gus sits forward with his head in his hands.

"I don't understand," Graylin says, weeping. "Why can't I go home? I didn't do anything. Why are they doing this to me?"

I embrace him in a tight hug. I have no words to soothe him. Jenny doesn't either.

Martinez approaches the defense table. He avoids making eye contact as he hands Jenny a document. "Since the picture of Kennedy has gone viral, we're amending the charges."

Jenny starts reading it as I glance over her shoulder.

"You're adding distribution of child pornography *and* invasion of privacy charges?" Jenny says. "Really? You have no evidence to support these charges. What kind of game are you playing?"

Martinez shifts his weight from one foot to the other. "No game at all. The D.A.'s Office is serious about sending a strong message to perpetrators of child pornography no matter how old they are."

Jenny glowers at him. "So what you're saying is, you're trying to make an example out of Graylin."

Martinez shrugs. "No. I'm just doing my job."

# CHAPTER 25

## *Graylin*

My head feels like it's going to blow up by the time I get back to my unit. I'm lying down in my cell—I don't care what they say, it's a cell, not a room—when Mr. Dennison announces that dinner's here.

I walk into the day room and stand in line to pick up a plate. All the kids are happy because we're having pepperoni pizza. I like pizza, but I'm mad at that judge for not letting me go home. I don't care what my attorneys say, this is all Crayvon's fault. He should be the one in here, not me.

"You Graylin, right?"

I turn around to see a tall kid with dreadlocks who looks at least fifteen or sixteen.

"How do you know my name?" I can't handle another bully messing with me so if I have to beat him up too, I will.

"You got a lot of props for going toe-to-toe with Tyke last night. Everybody around here is scared of him. Except me, of course."

I want to tell him that I'm scared of Tyke too. Instead, I turn around and wait for my pizza.

"They moved Tyke to the other side of the unit and put me over here so y'all can't fight no more. But you still gotta watch your back cuz he'll come at you again."

"I don't care." And I don't. I don't care about nothing anymore.

Kemal, a boy who was tight with Tyke is throwing me shade. Just to show I'm not scared, I get my pizza and sit down right across from him.

"Tyke want you to know it ain't over," Kemal whispers. "He still gonna kick your ass."

I'm about to tell him to bring it on when someone cuts me off.

"Tyke ain't gonna do nothin' to nobody," says the boy who was talking to me in line. "If Tyke got a beef with Graylin, then he got a beef with me. And what about you? You got a beef with me?"

Kemal shakes his head about ten times. "Naw, man, I'm just the messenger." He slides down to the far end of the bench.

"You good now," the boy says, sitting down next to me. "I got your back."

"Thanks," I mumble.

"My pops told me to have your back. He's friends with your Uncle Dre. They go way back. They both OG's."

I'm so relieved I almost want to kiss him. "What's your name?"

"Dontay. But they call me Little Slice on the street."

"Why do they call you that?"

"Because if you cross me, I'll slice you up into tiny little pieces." Little Slice laughs, but I don't.

"Look, I'ma keep it one hundred with you. If you wanna keep these dudes off your ass, you gotta act tough. You kicked Tyke's ass, but you walkin' around here lookin' like a little pussy. You gotta man up."

I want to ask Little Slice how I'm supposed to do that, but I don't want to look like a punk.

"What you locked up for?" he asks me.

"They said I had child pornography on my phone."

"Dude, that's messed up. Three of my boys got locked up for that. Your public defender probably don't even care about your case."

"I don't have a public defender. My dad hired me two lawyers."

"So what you gonna do about your case?"

"What do you mean? What can I do?"

Little Slice starts smiling like he knows a big secret. "You can do a lot. In fact, I know how to guarantee you don't get convicted cuz I got all kinda connections."

I can tell Little Slice likes to brag and act all hard, so I let him.

"So did you send that girl a picture of your penis or did she sext you?"

"I didn't sext nobody!"

Little Slice leans back. "Hold up, little bruh. I was just askin'. Turn down the volume."

"My attorneys are going to get me off."

"Believe that lie if you want to. I don't trust attorneys. They never tell you the real deal. They in it for the money."

I don't know for sure about Ms. Jenny, but I know Ms. Angela's not like that. I need to stop talking to Little Slice because he's making me depressed.

"You oughta let me help you," he says.

"How?"

"Just kick back and let me work my magic. What's the girl's name?"

I hesitate.

"Dude, you can trust me. My pops told me to look out for you."

"Kennedy Carlyle."

"Does she go to your school?"

"Yeah."

"What's the name of your school?"

I hesitate again.

"Do you want my help or not?" Little Slice says.

"Um, Marcus Preparatory Academy."

"Dang, bruh, you gotta be rich *and* smart to go there."

"I'm not rich. I got a scholarship."

"You think she sent that picture to you?" Little Slice asks. "Some of these ho's are scandalous."

"I think my best friend Crayvon sent it to me. But I don't know for sure."

"Aw, that's cold if one of your boys set you up like that."

"I'ma talk to my peeps and handle things for you."

"How are you gonna do that?"

"Just trust me, bruh. I got you."

# Chapter 26

## *Martinez*

The Carlyles are twenty minutes late for our meeting. When I enter the conference room, I find Kennedy protectively wedged between her parents. She's going to make a very sympathetic witness. The girl's eyes are sad and she can't make eye contact for more than a second or two. She's wearing the pain of Graylin Alexander's violation like a fresh coat of paint.

"Thanks for coming down," I begin. "I'm—"

"It's not like we had much of a choice." Simone's voice is infused with sarcasm. "You ordered us down here like *we're* the criminals."

I don't take her bait. "I'm still waiting for the forensics on Graylin Alexander's phone. I'd like to come out to your home sometime this week with my investigator. We want to simulate taking a picture through Kennedy's bedroom window to give us an idea of where he was standing when he invaded your daughter's privacy."

"Since you have to come out to the house anyway, why couldn't you interview her there?" Simone wants to know. "It's not like the case is going to trial tomorrow."

I don't care for Simone Carlyle. Fortunately, I'm very good at dismissing people I don't like.

"I'd like to begin by asking Kennedy a few questions." I take out the photograph, but don't slide it across the table yet. "This is an enlargement of the picture we found on Graylin's phone."

The girl's eyes dart over to the picture, then back down at the table.

"I want you to see it because I'm hoping you can provide some details about when it might've been taken. Can you handle it?"

It takes a moment, but Kennedy nods.

When I hand her the picture she glances at it, winces, then looks away.

"Can you confirm that's you in the picture?"

"Yes," Kennedy says meekly.

"Do you recognize where it was taken?"

"It looks like my bedroom." Her eyes return to the picture, remaining there a little longer this time. "So he was peeking in my bedroom window?"

"Yes, he was," her mother says, answering a question that wasn't addressed to her.

I study Kennedy's reaction. She doesn't say more, at least not in words. A tear slides down the right side of her face. "That picture is all over the Internet. It's so embarrassing."

I want to give Kennedy a chance to compose herself, so I turn to her parents. "Is Kennedy in counseling yet?"

For the first time, Simone drops her icy glare. Percy tugs at the cuffs of his monogrammed shirt.

"Not yet," Simone says. "We're still looking for the right therapist."

"I'm okay," Kennedy ekes out in a squeaky voice. "I don't want to talk to some stranger."

The Carlyles' delay in getting their daughter into counseling concerns me. The girl needs professional help to deal with this violation.

"Do you have any idea when the picture might've been taken?" I ask.

Simone interrupts. "How would she know—"

I hold up my hand. "I need Kennedy to respond."

Her eyes still avoid the picture. "I don't know."

"It looks like you're about to get dressed."

She steals another quick peek. "I think maybe I'd just gotten out of the shower."

"Do you shower in the morning or at night?"

"Both."

"Which do you do most often?"

"Evenings, I guess."

"Do you normally stand in front of the window to get dressed?"

Her eyebrows fuse into one. "But I wasn't standing in front of the window."

"I'm sorry. What I should've said is do you normally get dressed in your bedroom or the bathroom?"

"Mostly in my bedroom."

"There's a pink sweater lying on the bed. Do you remember wearing that sweater recently?"

Kennedy's pensive expression tells me she's trying to remember. "It's one of my favorites. I wear it a lot."

"Can you remember the last time?"

Kennedy hunches her shoulder. "I'm not sure."

"I'd like you to think about it some more when you get home. And if you remember, please call me."

She nods.

"Do you know if Graylin Alexander knows where you live?"

"Yeah. I've seen him on my block before. He's best friends with Crayvon, who lives up the street."

Six pairs of eyes zoom in on Kennedy. "When was the last time you saw Graylin on your street?"

"I don't know. He's at Crayvon's house all the time."

"Do you know if you saw him during the week he was arrested?"

Kennedy squints. "Probably."

"Was it on a school day or a weekend day?"

"A school day."

"Do you remember if it was during the day or night?"

"It was probably after school."

"Did you talk to him when you saw him?"

"No."

"Did you talk to his friend Crayvon?"

"No."

"What were they doing?"

"Walking down the street."

"Have you ever seen Graylin or Crayvon in your backyard?"

"No."

"Do you know if Graylin has a crush on you?"

Kennedy frowns. "No. I barely know him. But a lot of girls like him."

"Can you tell me which girls?"

Kennedy rattles off five names, which I quickly scribble down.

"Were any of them his girlfriends?"

"I don't know."

"Have any girls told you about"—I temper my words, fearing a hostile reaction from Mrs. Carlyle—"being with Graylin?"

"Being with him?" The girl looks confused.

What I want to know is whether young Graylin Alexander is sexually active. I'm about to ask her that question when I remember what the kids call it now. "Have you ever heard of him smashing any girls at your school?"

The two adult Carlyles look more confused than Kennedy was a second ago. I'm relieved when they don't ask for a translation.

Kennedy blushes. "No."

I suspect I'm not getting the truth. I need to know the real deal without Kennedy filtering the facts for her parents. "Is it okay if I take a few minutes and talk to Kennedy alone?"

Simone folds her arms across her chest. "Absolutely not."

I rub my eyes with my thumb and index finger, then stare across the table at Mr. Carlyle. "As an attorney, I'm sure you understand the need for me to get honest responses. Kennedy might be likely to speak more candidly without the two of you present."

Simone grimaces. "Kennedy, is that true? Would you feel better talking to the prosecutor without us here?"

Kennedy shakes her head. "No. I'm okay if you're here."

"We have a very open relationship," Simone says with a satisfied smirk. "Our daughter tells us everything."

*Lady, if you only knew.* I hear that delusional statement from parents so often it no longer fazes me. Kids don't tell their parents a thing. I certainly didn't and neither did they.

I know I won't gain any ground if I push any harder right now, so I don't. I ask a few more questions about Graylin, then end the meeting.

The Carlyles have been gone for almost fifteen minutes when the door to the conference room bursts open and all three of them bolt back inside.

"Kennedy just confided something to us," Simone says, her face flush. "Something you need to address A-S-A-P!"

I stand up. "What happened?"

"Go ahead, baby," Simone says, "tell them."

Kennedy opens her mouth, but only a sob comes out. She collapses into her mother's arms.

"You were right," Simone says. "Kennedy *doesn't* tell us everything. That boy had somebody call my baby last night and threaten her to drop this case. If that doesn't prove he's guilty, nothing will."

# CHAPTER 27

## *Graylin*

I get excited when I find out my attorneys are here to visit me. I didn't even know they were coming today. Nobody in my unit gets as many visitors and phone calls as I do.

When I step into the room, I know something bad has happened because Ms. Jenny and Ms. Angela have sad faces. I'm wondering if they're going to tell me that prosecutor has already convicted me. My dad is on speakerphone, which gets me even more worried.

"What's the matter, Ms. Jenny? Is something wrong?"

"We're here because somebody called Kennedy at home and threatened her. Was it you?"

I shake my head. I didn't do it, but I know who did.

Ms. Jenny is staring me down like she's trying to tell whether I'm lying. "Did you ask anyone to call Kennedy?"

"No. I swear I didn't."

"Do you know who might have called her?"

I rub my hands together. "Um, yeah. My friend Little Slice said he would take care of things for me. But I didn't know he was going to do that."

"Who the hell is Little Slice?" my dad yells. "I told you them thugs in there ain't your friends!"

I flinch. I almost forgot my dad was on the phone.

"He's in my unit. His real name is Dontay. His dad and Uncle Dre are friends. He's been looking out for me. That's the only reason nobody bothers me anymore."

Ms. Jenny asks me a whole bunch of questions about Little Slice. She asks me to repeat all of my conversations with him word for word. She says what Little Slice did has made things worse for me.

I don't understand how things can be worse since I didn't do anything.

"Certain charges make it possible for the prosecutor to transfer your case out of juvenile court," Ms. Jenny says. "Intimidating a witness is one of those charges. The prosecutor has filed a motion to have you tried as an adult."

"Are you friggin' kidding me?" my dad yells.

I don't understand how I can be tried as an adult when I'm a kid. "Why do they want to do that?"

"So they can put you in an adult prison!" my dad shouts.

I don't say anything for a long time because I'm still trying to understand. "But I'm only fourteen."

"They wouldn't put a fourteen-year-old in an adult prison," Ms. Angela says, then turns to Ms. Jenny. "He'd still go to the California Youth Authority, right?"

She nods. "Yeah. And it's not called the Youth Authority anymore. Now that they're under the Department of Corrections, it's the Division of Juvenile Justice."

My dad is so mad it sounds like he might have a heart attack. "I don't care what they call it. It's still prison!"

"But I didn't threaten anybody."

"The prosecutor claims that you asked Little Slice to do it," Ms. Jenny says.

"But I didn't. Why can't I just tell the judge that?"

"That's not going to fix it, Graylin," Ms. Jenny says, her voice extra soft. "Now we have to have what's called a fitness hearing. The judge will decide if your case should be transferred to adult court."

"This ain't right! You also told us he'd be going home!" my dad shouts at her through the phone, even though it was Ms. Angela, not Ms. Jenny who said that. "And now you're telling me they're gonna try my son as an adult. What in the hell am I paying you twenty grand for?"

Ms. Jenny starts saying a lot of stuff to calm down my dad, but it's not working. I'm not listening anymore because I can't stop staring at Ms. Angela. She's not saying anything and that's freaking me out. Ms. Angela is always telling me everything's going to be okay. Now, she won't even look at me.

When I get back to my unit, I go straight to my room. I'm really, really mad. At everybody. Especially Little Slice. I don't understand how that prosecutor can do this to me when all I did was save a stupid picture to my phone.

During recreation time, I find a bench where I can sit by myself. Yesterday, when my granny called, she said she was praying for me three times a day and told me to pray too. I close my eyes and look up at the sky. I try to pray, but I can't. I'm mad at God too.

I open my eyes and see Little Slice coming toward me. All I want to do is punch him in his face like I did Tyke.

He props his foot up on the bench. "What up, bruh?"

Ms. Jenny told me not to have any more conversations with Little Slice, but I can't help myself.

"You got me in trouble! You didn't tell me you were going to call Kennedy. You made my case worse!"

"Dude, what you talkin' 'bout?"

I tell him everything Ms. Jenny told me and how they're adding a new charge against me for intimidating a witness.

"Hold up, bruh. I didn't call that ho, but I did put one of my boys on it. What happened?"

"That prosecutor thinks I threatened her even though I didn't do anything!"

"Dude, that ho is lying. My peeps know what to say and what not to say."

"Well, I'm the one in trouble now. That prosecutor is trying to get me tried as an adult."

"Whoa. That prosecutor's going deep in your ass."

I want to sock him in the jaw.

"But if I was you, I'd be glad. At least now you have a chance of gettin' off."

I look at him like he's crazy. "You're buggin'."

"No, I'm serious. If you get transferred to adult court," Little Slice says, "your peeps can post bail and get you outta here. But the best thing is you get to have a jury. I'd rather go with a jury than a juvie judge any day. Ninety-nine percent of the time a kid loses in juvie court cuz the judge decides everything. But if you have a jury, all you need is one juror to believe you and you get off with a hung jury. So I don't know why you lookin' so sad."

I replay everything Little Slice just said. I *would* be better off with a jury. If I testify, I can tell them that I didn't do it. All I have to do is get a few mothers or even some teachers on the jury. When they find out I'm a good student, they'll believe me.

"I can see the wheels spinning in your big water head," Little Slice says, laughing. "But I'm tellin' you right now, your attorneys are gonna fight you on this. They ain't gonna want you to be tried as an adult."

"My attorneys told me I get to make all the decisions about my case."

"Yeah, but they ain't gonna be down with this," Little Slice continues. "Your pops either. But you gotta stand up for yourself. You feel me?"

What Little Slice is saying makes sense. I *would* be better off in adult court. And that's exactly where I'm going.

# CHAPTER 28

## *Graylin*

As one of the staff leads me to the attorney meeting room, I can hardly walk. My legs feel as flimsy as a bowl of Ramen noodles. I know Ms. Angela and Ms. Jenny won't agree with what I have to say, but this is *my* case and *my* life. So I'm going to do this *my* way.

When I enter the room and see my dad, I freeze.

"Hey, Little Man." My dad pulls me into a bear hug. "Angela got special permission for me to visit you today."

I'm not sure I can do this with my dad present. At least he's in a good mood. For now.

"Have a seat, Graylin." Ms. Jenny pulls out a chair for me. "We wanted to meet with you and your father to prepare you for the fitness hearing."

I suddenly have a headache. Probably because of what I have to do.

"During a fitness hearing," Ms. Jenny says, "the prosecutor has to prove that you can't be rehabilitated by the juvenile system. And if you can't, your case will be transferred to adult court."

I peer over at my dad. He looks as puzzled as I am.

"So how do they figure that out?" my dad asks.

"The judge will look at things like the type of crime, the child's criminal history, the potential for the child to improve and the seriousness of the crime. It's all about whether the judge thinks the kid is such a hopeless case, that he should be treated like an adult."

"Why do I need to be rehabilitated when I didn't do anything in the first place?" I ask, but nobody answers my question.

"That sounds like a piece of cake for us then." My dad is acting so happy. "My son's not some thug."

"Nothing is a piece of cake where the legal system is concerned," Ms. Jenny says, then glances at Ms. Angela as if it's her turn to speak. There's a short pause before she does.

"There's something else we need to advise you of," Ms. Angela says, mainly to my dad. "If Graylin is convicted on the pornography charges, be it juvenile or adult court, he'll have to register as a sex offender."

"What does that mean?" I ask.

My dad's not happy anymore. His face is all scrunched up. "It means they're saying you're a pedophile, which is bull!"

I don't even know what a pedophile is.

Ms. Angela turns to me. "Registering as a sex offender means you'll have to comply with certain requirements. For instance, every year, you have to advise local law enforcement of your address, where you go to school and where you work, so they can keep track of you at all times. You also have to provide your DNA."

"And don't it mean he can't even be alone around kids?" my dad says angrily.

All of this is confusing. How can I not be around other kids when I'm a kid myself? "Why would they want to keep track of me like that?"

My dad doesn't let Ms. Angela answer my question.

"So they can publish your name on a list of perverts!" I can see the veins in his forehead popping out. "Anybody can go on a computer and look at the list. So no college is going to accept you and nobody's going to rent you an apartment and no company is ever going to hire you because people don't want to work with a pervert. So what it really means is that you're screwed for life." My dad lowers his head and wipes his hand down his face.

I wait for Ms. Angela and Ms. Jenny to say my dad is over-reacting, but they don't.

I can't believe this. "Just because I saved Kennedy's picture on my phone?"

Ms. Angela nods.

"How long will I have to be a sex offender?"

Ms. Angela looks away.

"Possibly, forever," Ms. Jenny says.

My dad starts bouncing his knee up and down like I do when I get nervous or upset. "That's nuts! He's only fourteen. Every day it feels like we're walking deeper and deeper into a nightmare."

"This is only if there's a conviction," Jenny says, trying to make it sound like it's not a big deal. "Even if he's convicted, we might be able to get his record expunged if he doesn't get into trouble again. But you can only apply for that seven years after a conviction."

"Thanks," my dad says. "Now we have something to look forward to."

I still don't understand why anyone would do this to a kid just for having a naked picture. How can they convict me for something I didn't even know was against the law?

"We're going to fight this fitness hearing with everything we've got," Ms. Jenny says.

I take a deep breath and blurt out, "I don't want to fight it."

A puzzled look glazes my dad's face. "What? What're you talking about? Of course you do."

I try to remember everything Little Slice told me. "In juvie court, kids get convicted ninety-nine percent of the time because a judge decides everything. It's better for me to be in adult court because I get to have a jury. I'll only need one juror to believe me and I can get a hung jury and get off."

My dad is staring at me so hard I can almost feel his gaze touch my skin. "What? That's crazy. We ain't taking that kind of chance."

"Little Slice said—"

"Don't you ever mention that fool's name to me again!" my dad yells. "That thug's got you in enough trouble as it is. Don't you understand that?"

Ms. Angela holds up her hands. "Gus, please calm down. Shouting at him isn't helping the situation."

I'm glad Ms. Angela's on my side, so I focus only on her. "I want to take my chances in adult court. I want a jury. And in adult court I can also get out on bail."

"Boy, you don't know what you're talking about!"

"Little Slice told me you would try to talk me out of it. But this is my life and this is what I want to do."

My dad's eyes are about to pop out of his head. "Boy, I'll—"

Ms. Jenny stands up. "Gus, let's take a breather and hear Graylin out."

"Hear him out, my ass! This boy is talking nonsense and you need to tell him that. If I have to knock some sense into him, I will."

I don't look at my dad. I'm trying to find the courage to do something else Little Slice told me to do, but the words are stuck in my throat.

"Let's discuss the pros and cons with Graylin," Ms. Jenny says, "and then—"

"Lady," my dad barks, "you must be out of your friggin' mind. There ain't no pros to this!"

My stomach feels like it's full of bricks. What I'm about to say next is really going to make my dad have a meltdown. But I don't have any other choice.

I swallow hard, then blurt out, "I want to talk to my attorneys alone."

My dad jumps to his feet and leans over me. His face is so twisted up he looks like a monster. "I ain't going nowhere! You don't know what the hell you're talking about! I'm here to protect your stupid ass!"

I turn to Ms. Jenny. "You told me in the beginning that I'm the client and that I get to make the decisions about my case. So that's what I'm doing." I stop and take a deep breath. "I want a private meeting with my attorneys."

"Boy, I'll—"

Ms. Angela grabs my dad's arm and pulls him across the room. "Gus, just give us a few minutes to talk to him alone. We'll work this out."

My dad acts like he didn't hear her. "What's wrong with you? Have you lost your mind? I want you to stay away from this Slice fool. He's filling your head with nonsense." He sneers at Ms. Jenny. "This is not my child. He's never been disrespectful like this. You need to get him out of this place!"

I stare down at the floor, too scared to look up at my dad.

"Gus, please." Ms. Angela is begging him now. "Step outside for a minute and let us talk to Graylin."

My dad jerks the doorknob so hard the window rattles. As soon as he's gone, I can breathe again.

Ms. Jenny starts to say something, but I cut her off. I don't want to hear what my attorneys have to say either.

"Don't invite my dad to our meetings anymore," I tell them. "I want to be tried as an adult so I can have a jury. And no matter what you say, I'm not going to change my mind."

# CHAPTER 29

## *Angela*

It takes some doing, but we finally convince Gus to go home and let us talk to Graylin alone. Jenny and I spend another hour with him, but he won't budge.

"But Graylin, if you're convicted," I say, "you could end up doing more time. You can't take that risk."

"But I'm not going to get convicted. All I have to do is get one juror to believe me and I'll get a hung jury."

I close my eyes and try to clear my head. This entire conversation is unnecessary. There's no way the judge would send a kid with Graylin's spotless record to adult court.

"We want you to sleep on this, Graylin," Jenny says. "We'll talk to you again tomorrow."

"I'm not going to change my mind."

Jenny pats him on the back. "That's fine. We'll still talk tomorrow."

Once a staff member shows up to escort Graylin back to his unit, I stand up and press my forehead against the wall.

"Having an adult client who won't accept my legal advice is one thing," I say. "But having to wrestle with this naïve child who doesn't understand that he could be throwing his life away scares me to death."

"I think he's a very gutsy little guy," Jenny says.

I spin around. "What? How can you say that?"

"He's right about the juvenile system. A lot of judges are so jaded they think a kid is guilty as charged even before he walks into the courtroom. And with Martinez piling on the charges and Kennedy's parents pushing the way they are, he doesn't have much of a chance."

I can't possibly be hearing her correctly. "So what are you saying?"

"I'm saying he does have a better chance in the adult system. Even on the possession charge."

"Are you nuts?"

"There'll certainly be a few parents on his jury. They're going to look at Graylin's record and see that he's a good kid. They're going to see their kids in him and it's going to scare the heck out of them because under the same circumstance, their kid would've done the same thing he did."

"It's too much of a risk. If his case is transferred to adult court, we might as well walk him over to juvie prison right now."

"I hear you're an amazing attorney. Adult court is your domain. I think you can get him off."

"He can't win on the possession charge. He had the picture on his phone. How can I get him off?"

Jenny smiles and waits a beat. "Jury nullification. No matter what the law says, no jury will want to lock up a great kid like Graylin just for saving a picture on his phone."

"Have you lost your mind? That's a complete crapshot."

"Parents have no idea prosecutors are going after kids for this. The jury will be outraged. All we need is one juror to ignore the law and go with his gut and Graylin walks."

"It's fine for you to propose all these what-ifs, but if Graylin was your kid, I doubt you'd be supporting this."

"Whether he's in juvenile court or adult court, the stakes are the same," Jenny says. "If he's convicted, he's going to have to register as a sex offender, possibly for the rest of his life. He has a better shot in adult court because I don't think the prosecutor can find twelve people willing to convict him."

I cup my forehead. "If they think he took that picture, they'll convict him."

"But he didn't take the picture and the prosecution won't be able to prove that he did."

"You can't say that. We don't know what evidence they have."

Jenny rears back. "Are you saying you think he took it?"

"No. But I've been practicing law long enough to know that just because somebody's innocent doesn't mean they won't be convicted."

"I know this is a very scary roll of the dice," Jenny insists, "but at least there's a chance."

"No way. What Graylin wants to do is crazy, and his father agrees. So we're going to fight like hell at that fitness hearing."

"Gus isn't the deciding factor here. Graylin's our client, not Gus."

"Graylin's a naïve kid who thinks life is fair. I'm not letting him destroy his life."

Jenny reaches for her satchel, pulls out a book and starts flipping pages. "The juvenile court rules are crystal clear on this." She has the audacity to start reading to me like I'm a first-year law student.

*Role of counsel: An attorney's ethical allegiance is to the child and not to the parent or guardian paying you for representation. Parents are not allowed to waive rights for their*

*children since they may have conflicting interests. Parents*
*also need not be present when lawyers interview clients and*
*cannot be present if the child objects. The lawyer is ethically*
*required to present the child's position to the court.*

She slams the book down on the desk.

"Screw the rules!" I say. "Graylin's a fourteen-year-old kid who's getting bad advice from some fool in juvenile hall. It's our job to do what's best for him, regardless of what he wants."

"Did you just hear what I read? It's our job to follow our client's wishes."

"You're talking theory. I'm talking real world. A jury might be hesitant to lock up a fourteen-year-old white kid, but it's a different ball game for a black kid. And I'm not taking that kind of chance. The stakes are way too high."

A curtain of red inches up Jenny's neck. "So you're making this a race thing?"

"No, I'm making this a reality thing."

Both of us are so worked up we have to pause to catch our breaths.

"Just so I'm clear," I say, "are you telling me you're not going to fight to keep Graylin in juvenile court?"

Jenny's hands are gripping her narrow hips and she's sneering at me. "I'm going to do what my client asks me to do."

"If you're not going to do what's best for Graylin, he may not be your client anymore."

Jenny snatches her book and stuffs it back into her satchel. "I'm pretty sure Graylin wants an attorney who's complying with his wishes," she says with a cunning smile. "So if anybody's getting removed from this case, it's you, not me."

# Chapter 30

## *Graylin*

I finish my breakfast and wait in the day room. My fitness hearing starts in one hour. I'm nervous, but I'm ready to do what I have to do.

My Uncle Dre spent two hours with me yesterday, trying to convince me that I don't want my case transferred to adult court. I finally said okay, just so he would leave.

Little Slice comes up to me in the day room and slaps me on the back.

"You good to go?"

I nod, but I'm really not.

"Do what I told you to do and everything'll go down just like I said it would. And when you win your case, you gonna owe me."

One of the staff walks me and two other boys across the covered walkway that connects juvenile hall to the courthouse. Ms. Angela and Ms. Jenny are waiting for me. Both of them have sour looks on their faces like they're mad at somebody. Probably me.

Ms. Angela stands up and gives me a hug. "Dre told me you guys talked for a long time yesterday. So are you ready to fight this fitness hearing?"

"Yep."

Ms. Angela looks over at Ms. Jenny and smirks. "Good. I'm glad we're on the same page."

I'm sorry that I'm going to have to hurt Ms. Angela's feelings. But this is my life, not hers.

Ms. Jenny comes over and hugs me too.

"Just like at the detention hearing, you need to remember that the judge is watching you," Ms. Angela says. "So sit up straight and be respectful. It's more important than ever that the judge gets to see the kind of person you are. We know you're a great kid. We want the judge to know it too."

"Yeah, okay."

"And say *yes*, not *yeah*," Ms. Angela corrects me.

I want to roll my eyes, but instead I say, "Yes, Ms. Angela."

When we enter the courtroom, I see my dad and Uncle Dre sitting on the back row.

*W-T-F!*

My granny and my aunt Macie are here too! Why'd he have to bring them today of all days? I hurry to the front of the courtroom without even looking at them.

The asshole prosecutor is already at his table. If my eyes could shoot bullets, I'd put a dozen holes in his head right here in the middle of this courtroom. He's trying to put me in prison for nothing and I wish he would die.

The bailiff asks everyone to stand as Judge Miller takes the bench. Everyone stands up, except me.

Ms. Angela glares down at me and whispers, "What's wrong with you? Get up!"

I ignore her.

Ms. Jenny is peering down at me too. They must think I'm wigging out, but they haven't seen nothing yet.

Ms. Angela squeezes my shoulder, but I still don't move. "Graylin, what are you doing? Stand up!"

The judge props an elbow on her desk. "Ms. Ungerman, is there a reason your client is disregarding the bailiff's instruction to stand?"

"Yeah," I shout out, "cuz I don't want to."

Dead silence follows my words. It's as if somebody waved a magic wand and everybody is frozen in place.

Judge Miller narrows her eyes and wags her finger at me. "Young man, do you understand the seriousness of this hearing?"

"Yeah, I do. And it's a bunch of bull, so I ain't participating." I fold my arms and slide down so low in my chair that my chin almost touches the table.

When I see Ms. Angela turn around and stick out her arm toward the back of the room, I know that's a signal for my dad. He wants to run up here and strangle me. But I'm not worried because I know the bailiff won't let him.

"Young man, the disrespect you're showing in my courtroom is totally unacceptable. Would you please stand?"

"Ain't no reason for me to stand cuz we don't need to have no fitness hearing," I shout at the judge. "I want to be tried as an adult. So go ahead and send me to adult court cuz I ain't staying here to get railroaded for something I didn't do."

Jenny's face is so red it looks like she got stung by a zillion bumblebees.

Nobody's saying anything, so I keep talking. "I want justice my way. I wanna be in adult court with a jury of my peers."

"Your Honor," Ms. Jenny sputters. "May we approach?"

"Counselor, that sounds like an excellent idea."

Both of my attorneys and the prosecutor almost tumble over each other getting up to the bench. They're trying to talk low, but I can hear everything they're saying.

Ms. Jenny opens her mouth to say something, but Ms. Angela cuts in.

"Your Honor, since our client's been detained at juvenile hall, he's been unduly influenced by another juvenile there. That juvenile has convinced him that he'd be better off in adult court because he'd be entitled to a jury. And he's convinced that a jury won't convict him. We've tried to talk to him, but he won't listen. Please excuse his behavior today. This is all an act."

Ms. Jenny isn't saying anything. Her arms are crossed and her head is cocked to the side.

The stupid prosecutor throws up his hands. "Well, if the boy's own attorneys can't control him, the juvenile system certainly can't rehabilitate him."

Judge Miller frowns. "Have you explained to your client the consequences of what could happen to him if this case is transferred to adult court?"

Ms. Angela and Ms. Jenny nod at the same time. "Repeatedly," Ms. Angela says.

The judge drums her fingers on a stack of papers on her desk. "From what I know of this young man's background, this is not a situation where I feel the minor should be sent to adult court." She eyes the prosecutor. "So unless Mr. Martinez puts on an unusually strong case, that's unlikely to happen. But the conduct he's displaying in my courtroom right now is very troubling and might cause me to change my mind."

"Your Honor, can we have a short break to speak with our client?" Ms. Angela says.

The judge checks her watch. "I'll give you twenty minutes. But if your client comes back in here acting like this, I might be inclined to grant his wish."

# CHAPTER 31

## *Gus*

As soon as we're behind closed doors, I explode. "What the hell is wrong with you? You have no idea what you're doing!"

Graylin slouches down further in his chair, his hands clasped.

"Sit up straight and look at me!"

He takes his time sitting up. His eyes are focused on the wall to my left, not on me.

"Please lower your voice," Jenny warns me. "We don't want one of the deputies coming in here. And it's not helping things when you yell at him. We need to talk this out."

I swing around to face Jenny. "Lady, there ain't nothing for us to talk about. My son is black. He don't get the same chances a white kid might get. I'm handling this my way, not yours. And he's gonna do what I tell him to do. Even if I have to beat his ass to make him do it."

"But I can get a jury in adult court," Graylin pleads, "Little Slice said—"

"I don't care what that fool said. Do you understand that you're facing felony charges? You're gonna go back into that courtroom and act like you got some home training. I didn't raise you this way."

Graylin flies out of his chair and stands chest-to-chest with me. Both of our faces are distorted with rage.

"This ain't your life! It's *my* life!" Graylin's eyes are glassy with tears. "That judge is going to lock me up for something I didn't do. I want a jury trial. At least that way I'll have a chance to show them I'm innocent. I don't have a chance in here. You're always telling me to man up. Well, that's what I'm doing. I'm being a man. And a man makes his own decisions."

I'm momentarily stunned into silence by my son's defiance. Before I can respond, Angela steps between us.

"Let's all calm down." She grabs Graylin by the arm and pulls him away. "I'm going to ask for a continuance."

Graylin jerks away from her. "I don't want a continuance. I'm not going to change my mind and nobody in this room can make me!"

I reach around Angela and try to grab my son, but he jumps back out of my reach. "Boy, are you—"

"Both of you cut it out!" Jenny yells. "Let's give Graylin a few minutes alone to think about what he's about to do."

Angela tugs me toward the door and Jenny follows. We walk a few feet down the hallway, away from the clusters of parents and kids waiting for their cases to be heard. "When we go back into court," Angela says, "we need to press the judge hard for her help. Maybe she'll do the right thing despite Graylin's behavior."

Jenny exhales. "But that's not what Graylin wants."

"Screw what Graylin wants!" I fume. "What are you going to say to me when my fourteen-year-old son gets locked up?"

Everyone in the hallway is staring at us now. I'm surprised that one of the sheriff's deputies hasn't come over.

"If you're going to prevent me from following Graylin's wishes," Jenny says, "then I'll have to resign from the case."

I spread my hands, palms up. "See ya."

Jenny starts to walk away, but Angela stops her. "Wait! This is not the time for you to bail. Graylin needs you in there. Both of you need to chill!"

When I see the bailiff walking toward us, I assume he's about to tell us to quiet down. Instead he says, "Judge Miller wants everybody back in the courtroom."

# CHAPTER 32

## *Angela*

When we return to the courtroom, Martinez is sitting on the edge of the prosecution table. The judge is standing nearby. She's not wearing her robe.

"Did you two work things out with your client?" the judge asks.

Her question is directed at Jenny, but I'm the one who responds. "Your Honor, we can't seem to get him to change his mind."

The judge marches over to where Graylin is standing and pins him with a look intense enough to spark a fire.

"Young man, do you understand what you're doing?"

Graylin has resumed his gangbanger persona. His arms are locked across his chest and his head is arrogantly cocked to the side. "Yep. I want me some justice."

His right leg is trembling, but he's otherwise staying in character.

"If you're convicted in adult court," Judge Miller tells him, "the consequences are much more serious. You could end up with multiple felonies on your record that might never go away. It's best for you to have your case heard in juvenile court."

"Sounds like you already decided to convict me," Graylin says, just as surly as before. "This is why we need Black Lives Matter cuz the black man keeps getting screwed over by the system. I said I don't wanna be here. So send me to adult court, damn it!"

The judge's pert lips flatten into a straight line.

I immediately start pleading Graylin's case. "Your Honor, my client is not himself. You've read the detention report. He's a great kid. This is an act. We'd like you to take into account that he's been influenced by—"

"Counselor, I don't care who influenced him," Judge Miller bristles. "If one of my sons talked to me like this, I'd—" She catches herself. "Well, that's beside the point."

"Your Honor," I continue, "he's pretending to—"

"I don't care if he's pretending. Your client's disrespectful behavior and his failure to listen to your advice tell me better than that detention report ever could that he's unfit for the juvenile justice system. So trying to rehabilitate him would indeed be a waste of this court's time. Since he wants to be in adult court, that's precisely where I'm sending him. Let me get my robe so we can put this on the record."

# CHAPTER 33

## *Angela*

Graylin is smiling like it's Christmas morning and Santa brought him everything on his wish list.

"Now I can get out on bail, right, Ms. Angela? Can I go home now?" He grins over at me with hopeful, glistening eyes.

I'm not a proponent of child abuse, but right now I want to slap him upside his big naïve head. He has no idea what he's just done. Gus storms out of the courtroom. I can hear his aunt and grandmother weeping as they trail behind him.

"No, Graylin, you can't go home now. Your case has to be transferred to adult court first. A Superior Court judge has to set bail."

"When is that going to happen?"

"It could take several days."

Shock rocks his face. "So I have to stay at juvenile hall until then?"

"Yes, you do. And there's no guarantee that the court's going to even let you out on bail."

He turns to Jenny as if she might contradict me. She meets his stunned eyes with silence.

Graylin's voice starts to quiver like he's about to cry. "But Little Slice said I would get out on bail."

"I guess this proves Little Slice doesn't know everything, huh?"

"But Little Slice said—"

"If you mention Little Slice to me one more time, I swear I'm going to slice *you* up into little pieces."

Graylin smiles. "That's funny, Ms. Angela."

"There's nothing funny about what you did. The first thing you need to do is apologize to your father for your behavior. He may not even want to post your bail."

For the first time, Graylin seems to realize that Gus is holding the keys to his freedom.

Martinez walks over. "It's been nice working with you, counselors. On the adult side, the case will be assigned to Lorelei Sullivan. Child pornography cases are her forte."

I want to slap Martinez upside the head too. "Thanks for everything."

Jenny picks up her satchel and is about to leave.

"Hold up," I say. "Why don't we have lunch? We need to clear the air."

Thirty minutes later, we're seated at a sandwich shop, not far from the courthouse. We place our orders and take seats until our food is ready.

"I'm sorry about getting so upset," I begin. "But I couldn't agree with you about letting Graylin make the decision on this."

Jenny hunches her shoulders. "Well, he did anyway. Now that you'll be in adult court, you'll be in familiar territory. Good luck."

What I'm about to say will no doubt come as a surprise to her. It's a surprise to me too. "I'd like you to stay on the case."

Jenny blinks.

"You know these sexting cases backward and forward," I continue. "I know the adult system. We'll make a great team."

"No, we won't. Even though he's in adult court, the same rules still apply. Graylin is the client and he gets to make the ultimate decisions. I'm not going to disregard my obligations to my client just because you want to act like his mother."

I remind myself that this is not about me. I need to do what's best for Graylin, and Graylin needs Jenny fighting for him. I need her too.

"I wasn't trying to act like his mother. I was trying to keep him from ruining his life. The fact that he thinks he did something good shows that he's not mature enough to make a decision like this."

Jenny looks away. Instead of convincing her that we can continue to work as a team, I've just reconfirmed that we'll still be tugging at opposite ends of the same rope.

Someone calls out my ticket number and I get up to retrieve my turkey sandwich. Jenny's number is called next. We both ignore the cloud of distrust hanging over us and start eating.

"If we can find out who took that picture and sent it to Graylin," I say after several bites, "I think we have a chance of getting him off. Even on the possession charge." I hope Jenny notices that I'm still using the plural *we*. "I didn't want to admit it before, but I do think we have a shot at jury nullification. Frankly, it's our best shot."

Jenny reaches for her phone. "I have an excellent investigator. Her name's Mei Lau. If anybody can find out who took that picture, she can. She's great at navigating in juvenile circles. Even though she's in her thirties, she could easily pass for fourteen or fifteen. I just texted you her contact information."

"I'm sure I can use her, but I also need you. Graylin does too. Will you please stay on the case?"

Rather than answer me, Jenny takes a bite of her sandwich. I put mine down and stare across the table at her. If I have to grovel for Graylin's sake, I will.

"Look, Jenny, let's make this about Graylin. Not about—"

"I don't know," she says. "Let me think about it and get back to you."

# CHAPTER 34

## *Angela*

As usual, arraignment court is a zoo. Being back in adult court fills me with a strange, yet familiar calm. This is *my t*erritory. I look toward the cage and spot Graylin in his gray sweat suit. He looks like a small ferret next to the five grown men in the cage with him. He waves at me. I don't wave back because that isn't allowed. There's a sign to that effect on the wall inside the cage.

When the judge calls Graylin's case, a deputy escorts him to the table where I'm standing.

"How are you doing?" I ask.

"I'm good," Graylin says, hugging me. "Can you get me out today, Ms. Angela?"

"Maybe."

I don't say any more than that because the truth would crush him. His aunt Macie agreed to put up her house. Assuming the judge grants bail, it could still be two or three days, maybe longer, before all the paperwork is processed.

"Your dad's supposed to be here," I say, looking over my shoulder.

"He's still mad at me. But when I win my trial, he'll understand."

I'm still mad at Graylin too. A fourteen-year-old can't drink, drive, smoke, vote or even sign a contract, but the law says he can make his own legal decisions? Whoever came up with that jewel was smoking something.

"When the judge asks how do you plead, say *not guilty* and not a word more," I tell him. "And you better not pull any of that disrespectful crap you did in juvenile court."

Graylin grins. "Okay, Ms. Angela. I won't."

The judge opens a folder, then stares down at me. "You're kidding me. Another sexting case? How old is the defendant?"

"Fourteen," I say.

The exasperation on the judge's face matches mine. "How do you plead?"

I give Graylin a nudge.

"Not guilty," he calls out in a loud, clear voice.

"My client has never been in trouble before. We'd like to ask that the defendant be released on O-R to his father. He'll be under twenty-four-hour supervision at home."

The judge turns to the prosecutor. "You okay with that?"

The deputy D.A. handling arraignments today is a fifty-plus, hard ass who plays it by the book. When I tried to talk to him earlier this morning, he said he didn't have time. I'm glad he won't be the prosecutor trying the case.

"We object, Your Honor," the prosecutor says. "The defendant's in adult court because he tried to intimidate a witness. We're asking that he remain in custody without bail."

*Without bail?* My heart starts to palpitate.

"Your Honor, that's unfairly excessive for a case of this nature. This young man is an excellent student with no prior criminal record. And the charge of witness intimidation is a farce."

The judge looks down at the papers on his desk. "Counselor, since a juvenile court judge sent his case here, he's obviously not the angel you want me to think he is."

The prosecutor interrupts. "I'd like to direct your attention to the judge's certification and the transcript of how disrespectfully the defendant behaved toward the court."

The judge pauses to read. "I see that here."

"In addition," the prosecutor continues, "the victim's mother is in court today. She'd like to see the defendant remain in custody because she fears for her daughter's safety."

All eyes turn to Simone Carlyle, who's dressed in black like she's here for a funeral. She stands up even though she wasn't asked to. Gus and Dre are sitting four rows behind her.

"Your Honor, I strongly disagree. I'm requesting house arrest, ankle monitoring and no computer access except for completion of his schoolwork, which will be supervised."

"I'll split the baby," the judge says. "Bail is granted at fifty thousand dollars. The defendant will also be under house arrest and required to wear an ankle monitor. Next case."

"Fifty thousand dollars!" Graylin looks as if he's about to crumple into tears. "My dad doesn't have that much money!"

"He only has to have a portion of it. Don't worry. We've already worked it out. I'll come back to talk to you after I speak with your father."

A deputy appears to escort Graylin away.

I motion Gus into the hallway and explain everything I need him to do regarding the bail. I'm about to head back inside when I see Jenny standing a few feet away.

"Nice job in there," she says.

She has no idea how happy I am to see her.

"So is this just a coincidence or can I interpret your being here as a good sign?"

Jenny smiles. "I'm in."

I give her a hug.

"What made you change your mind?"

"Good old-fashioned outrage. I'm sick and tired of the D.A.'s Office filing these cases and labeling good kids as sex offenders for the rest of their lives. I'm ready to help you kick some butt."

# CHAPTER 35

## *Angela*

Jenny and I are in my office waiting for her investigator to arrive. The three of us are going to discuss case strategy and outline the evidence we need to get Graylin acquitted.

There's a gentle knock on the door and a cute Asian girl with a nose ring and a purple streak in her bangs steps into the room. Jenny's right. Mei doesn't look anywhere close to thirty.

After introductions and some quick background on the case for Mei, we start tossing around ideas.

"We need someone else to point the finger at," Jenny says. "And that someone is the person who took the picture and sent it to Graylin."

"Are you certain it's the same person?" Mei asks.

Jenny stops to think. "I just assumed it was, but you make a good point."

"So you're confident your client didn't take it?"

"Yes," I say before Jenny can answer.

"I'll need to interview him." Mei scribbles something in her notebook. "He can help me figure out which of his classmates I should talk to."

"I can set that up," I say.

"Since the note was left at school," Mei continues as she examines it, "one of his classmates is probably involved. And it sounds like it was written by a kid."

I glance down at my copy and reread it.

*Dear Mrs. Keller,*

*Graylin Alexander should be ashamed of himself. He took a naked picture of Kennedy Carlyle with his iPhone. He also said he was going to beat her up and embarrass her by posting the picture on Instagram so it could go viral. Please stop him from doing this!*

*Signed, Anonymous*

I tug at a swatch of my hair. "I just wish we knew which kid."

"Don't worry," Jenny says. "Mei will find out. She's amazing."

Mei puts the note away and starts examining the photograph found on Graylin's phone. In the picture, Kennedy Carlyle appears to have been captured mid-stride in what looks like a bedroom. Her breasts and pubic area are clearly visible.

"Can't you argue that the picture doesn't meet the definition of obscenity under the statute?" Mei asks.

I reach for my iPad and reread California Penal Code Section 311.

*"Obscene matter" means matter that, to the average person, applying contemporary statewide standards, appeals to the prurient interest, that depicts or describes sexual conduct in a patently offensive way, and that lacks serious literary, artistic, political or scientific value.*

"Mei's right," I say. "That picture doesn't show any sexual conduct."

Jenny shakes her head. "I wish it was going to be that easy. When you read section 311 in conjunction with the section that defines sexual conduct, the picture does indeed fall within the statute."

"I'll take a look at Kennedy's social media pages as soon as I leave," Mei says. "That might give us some helpful information."

"Her pages are all shut down now," Jenny says. "But I took a look at her Snapchat, Instagram, Tumblr and Facebook pages the same day I got the case." She hands several pages to Mei. "Here are my notes and some screenshots. I wrote down the names of the kids who seemed to communicate with her the most."

Mei quickly scans them. "It amazes me that kids can find the time to manage all of these sites. Find anything interesting?"

Jenny shakes her head. "Kennedy Carlyle loves hot pink, owls, all things Paris and has a big-time crush on Drake and Katy Perry. My first thought after spending two hours on her social media pages was that she's a very nice little girl."

"So who does Graylin think sent him the picture?" Mei asks.

"His best friend Crayvon Little," Jenny says. "I didn't find anything helpful on his social media pages. And I don't know about motive, but he certainly had means and opportunity. Not only does he live on the same street as Kennedy, he just happens to have made a trip to the administration office right before a school clerk found the note lying on a counter. Unfortunately, no one saw him or anyone else put it there."

Mei asks for the spelling of Crayvon's name and writes it down.

"If we're going to win this," Jenny says, "we have to pull at the heartstrings of the jury. Every juror in that courtroom has to see their son, grandson, or nephew in Graylin and understand that the same thing could happen to them."

"How do you guys get around the possession charge since the picture was on Graylin's phone?"

"It's a specific intent crime," Jenny explains. "One argument we're going to make is that he lacked intent. While Graylin saved it to his phone, he didn't know it was pornography."

Mei frowns. "Ignorance of the law is no defense. Have you won with that argument before?"

"Nope. But there's always a first time."

"And you're sure Graylin's telling you the truth when he says he didn't take the picture?" Mei asks again.

"Yes," Jenny says. "There's a strong sense of righteous indignation in a child who's been falsely accused. I definitely see that in Graylin."

# Chapter 36

## *Mei*

My friends are always telling me I should be glad that I look half my age. Maybe I'll be grateful when I'm fifty, but right now, it's mostly annoying. Except when I'm trying to pass myself off as a middle-school student.

I knock on Crayvon Little's front door and wait for the response I've heard a million times.

Mrs. Little opens the door, looks me up and down and says, "You're the investigator? You don't even look old enough to drive."

I flash a smile that hides my irritation. "I assure you I am." I shake her hand and step into her living room.

Sharon Little is a thin, fair-skinned woman who wears her hair short and her attitude strong. She has the sturdy stance of a woman you don't mess with, despite her lithe frame.

"Crayvon's back there on that dang computer. He lives on that thing."

Mrs. Little yells down the hallway and a tall, waif-like kid bounces into the room dressed in jeans and an oversized Stephen Curry jersey.

"This is Ms. Lau, Graylin's investigator. She wants to see if you know anything that can help Graylin's case."

She takes a seat on the living room couch. Crayvon sits down next to her, while I settle into a cushy armchair.

"It's a shame what they're doing to that boy. Ruining his life for nothing. I don't believe for a minute that Graylin took a picture of that girl through her bedroom window. That boy is an angel. I heard that girl's mama is trying to throw the book at him. She better be careful because what goes around always comes right back to you. Go get Ms. Lau a bottle of water," she tells her son.

"Do you know Mrs. Carlyle?" I ask.

"Just in passing. The Carlyles have lived on this street for at least five years, but she barely waves and never participates in any of our block parties."

"Which house is it?" I ask, although I already know.

She steps over to the picture window. It's the beige house with the white trim four houses down on the opposite side of the street."

"Simone—that's the mother—thinks she's all that because she's a vice president at some company. Raised her daughter to think that too."

"Have you had much contact with Kennedy?"

"Not really. She keeps that child protected, too protected. Anyway, you're not here to talk to me."

Mrs. Little suggests that we move into the dining room. I don't object even though I prefer the more relaxed setting of the living room. A comfortable witness is a more talkative witness.

Crayvon hands me a bottle of water and places a coaster on the table. I start by asking him general questions about his classes. He isn't a shy kid, but he's not overly forthcoming either.

"Is everybody at school talking about the picture?"

"Yep."

"Have you seen it?"

He pauses as his eyes steal a glance at his mother.

"Go on, boy," Mrs. Little says. "I know you looked at it just like everybody else."

"Yeah, I've seen it."

"Who showed it to you?"

He pauses again. "Kenya."

"What's Kenya's last name?"

"Morris."

"Do you know how she got the picture?"

"From Instagram. But it's not up there anymore. Kenya saved it on her phone like Graylin did. A lot of people did. But when everybody started talking about Graylin getting arrested, they got scared and deleted it off their phones. Everybody saw it though. It went viral."

"Do you know who took the picture?"

"Nope."

"Do you know who posted it on Instagram?"

"Nope. But I know Graylin didn't. He wouldn't do that."

"Do you know of anybody who didn't like Kennedy and might've wanted to embarrass her?"

"Nope."

"Do you know of anybody who didn't like Graylin?"

"Nope. He's popular and really smart too. He always helps me with my algebra."

"Does Graylin ever come over to your house?"

"Yep."

"What do you guys usually do?"

He shrugs. "Mostly play Nintendo. Or just hang out."

The phone rings and Mrs. Little gets up to answer it.

"I understand that Kennedy lives across the street. Do you ever go over to her house?"

Crayvon freezes, then steals a glance down the hallway, where his mother is on the phone. "Um, no."

His stricken face sends off a warning signal. *He's lying.* If I'm going to get any admissions out of him, I need to do it before Mrs. Little returns.

"Have you and Graylin ever gone over to Kennedy's house when he came over to hang out with you?"

I include Graylin in my question so Crayvon thinks I'm focusing on Graylin's conduct, not his.

"Um," he tugs at a loose thread on the hem of his jersey, "not that I can recall?"

*Not that I can recall?* He sounds like a well-coached witness.

Before coming here, I looked up Kennedy's house on Google. Whoever shot the picture had to be standing outside her bedroom window. I lucked up and found pictures of the interior of the Carlyles' home on a real estate website. Those pictures and the Google Earth view show that the bedrooms are in the back on the ground floor, which means the picture taker had to enter the backyard.

"Have you and Graylin ever gone into Kennedy's backyard?"

Once again, Crayvon's face flashes panic. "Nope. Never."

"So you guys have never looked into Kennedy's bedroom window before?"

"Of course not. I wouldn't do that. Neither would Graylin."

Mrs. Little returns just as I'm asking my next question.

"Do you like Kennedy? I mean, as a friend?"

"Nope. Nobody likes her. She's too fake. Thinks she's all that because her parents buy her anything she wants. She has some Nikes that cost over four hundred dollars. Most girls don't care about expensive tennis shoes, but she tries to outdo the boys."

"She gets that snootiness from her mama," Mrs. Little chimes in.

"Does Kennedy have many friends?"

"Not really. She only hangs out with LaShay Thornton."

"Is LaShay in the eighth grade too?"

Crayvon nods.

"And you're sure you don't know who might've taken that picture of Kennedy?"

His eyes dart everywhere except in my direction. "Nope. I have no idea."

# CHAPTER 37

## *Sullivan*

The new case I received today makes me want to rethink my career choice. Graylin Alexander. Fourteen years old. No prior record. It's my job to put him away for possession of child pornography.

I flip through the detention report and frown. This boy reads like an angel. Stellar grades, a stable home life, and no record of truancy. The affidavits from his minister and teacher would qualify him for sainthood.

Picking up the phone, I dial Martinez's office.

"I just got the Graylin Alexander file. This kid doesn't belong in adult court. Even the detention report says so. How'd he end up on my desk?"

"The kid got it into his head that he'd be better off in adult court because he'd have a jury and his attorneys couldn't talk him out of it," Martinez explains. "He swore at the judge and started acting out, so she granted his wish."

A kid can't just act out and end up in adult court. Martinez had to file a motion for a fitness hearing. "Why'd you even push to have this kid tried as an adult? He's sounds like a choir boy."

"The parents of the girl are politically connected. I got an order to go for the jugular."

"Why?"

"They want to make an example out of this kid. That's why I filed the pornography charges as felonies rather than misdemeanors."

"Can we prove he took the picture?"

"We don't have any solid evidence of that yet, but he admitted to the police that he saved it from Snapchat. So, the possession charge is your clear winner. The witness intimidation charge isn't as solid, but it's still doable. Unless you can find some evidence to show he took the picture, the distribution and invasion of privacy charges are losers. I planned to drop them down the line anyway."

"What about the criminal threat charge? Is that based solely on the anonymous note?"

"Yeah. If no evidence turns up, you might have to drop that one too."

This is not how I operate. I don't file charges and then hope that the evidence to support them magically appears.

"What about the victim? Is she in bad shape? Suicidal or anything like that?"

"No."

"Thanks a lot for such a wonderful case."

Martinez chuckles.

I hang up and try to psyche myself up for this case. I miss the good old days when there were no cell phones, texts, tweets or kids posting provocative selfies online every five seconds.

Cases like this make me ultra-paranoid about keeping my own house in order. I open my laptop and dial into Net Nanny. Protecting my two kids and protecting my career go hand in hand. Considering what I do for a living, it would be more than embarrassing if one of my kids were accused of sexting.

I punch in my password and go through my son's texts, emails and social media accounts. I can see in real time everything he's doing online. At thirteen, Jonathan is still into video games and has recently become fascinated with rattlesnakes. As long as he doesn't bring one home, his new hobby is fine with me.

With a greater sense of trepidation, I switch over to my daughter's account. My fifteen-year-old is growing more and more obsessed with the number of likes she receives on Instagram. I've been giving serious thought to taking away Nina's cell phone and limiting her computer use to schoolwork. But I know from first-hand experience that the helicopter-parenting model is doomed to fail. I've sat across the table from far too many devastated parents who'd banned their kids from social media, only to find out that they used a friend's phone to access the Snapchat or Instagram account that landed them in court.

I quickly scan all of Nina's social media accounts, ending with Instagram. Finding nothing objectionable, I'm about to log off when I decide to click on the page of Brooke, Nina's best friend. The first picture that catches my attention is a shot of Nina, Brooke, and Zoey. All three girls are bent at the waist, looking back over their shoulders with puckered pink lips. They're wearing identical butt-exposing shorts—shorts I didn't buy for Nina—their tight little rear ends pointed directly at the camera. They might as well have written the caption *Mr. Pedophile, please come and get me!* underneath the picture.

I snatch the receiver from my desk phone, then slam it back into the cradle. I grab my keys and cell phone instead and head for the elevator. I need to have a talk with my darling little daughter in the safety of my car. It wouldn't look good for the deputy D.A. prosecuting Graylin Alexander to be overheard screaming at her daughter about her obscene Instagram picture.

# CHAPTER 38

## *Mei*

The day after my interview with Crayvon, I decide to return to his street to nose around Kennedy's house. I need to figure out how someone took that picture through her bedroom window.

I'm leaning toward siding with Graylin that Crayvon was the one who set him up. I haven't shared this with Angela or Jenny yet. I'd like to have something a little more concrete than a gut feeling before I finger Crayvon as our guy.

I park my Prius a few houses east of Kennedy's house and climb out carrying a clipboard and my Nikon. If anyone asks, I'm a photographer hired by a real estate agent to take pictures of homes in the area.

I approach Kennedy's house and knock lightly on the front door. When I get no answer, I ring the doorbell. To my relief, no one answers. I walk around to the side and see a gate leading into the backyard. I check to see if it's locked, but the latch opens easily.

After gazing over my shoulder to make sure no one is watching, I squeeze through the gate, waiting a second or two to make sure the Carlyles don't have a vicious guard dog, before going all the way inside. I snap a wide shot of the backyard, take a couple pictures of the two bedroom windows and scurry back out.

I'm almost at the end of the driveway when I notice a young girl sitting on the steps of a house across the street. I wave. The girl waves back.

"What's your name?" I ask, after crossing the street.

"Taisha."

"Why aren't you in school today?"

"I had a bad asthma attack this morning. But I'm better now. What were you doing in Kennedy's backyard?"

I wish the girl hadn't seen that. I act like a politician and pretend I didn't hear the question. "Do you know Kennedy Carlyle?"

"Yep."

"Since Kennedy lives right across the street, she must be a good friend of yours?"

The girl purses her lips. "We used to be best friends, but not no more. Now LaShay is her only friend. But I don't care. Kennedy's being homeschooled now. She's probably too embarrassed to go to school since everybody's talking about that naked picture of her."

"So you go to Marcus Prep?"

"No. You have to be rich to go there."

"Then how do you know about the picture?"

"Because everybody was talking about it in my Sunday school class."

"Where do you go to Sunday school?"

"Greater Mount Calvary."

"Did you see the picture?"

"Nope. I didn't wanna see it. You sure ask a lot of questions. You must be a private investigator working for Graylin. He goes to my church too."

I nod. This little girl is sharp.

"Do you know anybody who saw the picture?"

"Yeah, lots of people. It was all over Instagram. But it's gone now."

I don't buy her claim that she didn't want to see it. Since she knows that it's no longer on Instagram, that means she must've at least searched for it.

"Does anybody at your Sunday school know who took it?"

"Nope." She pauses. "But I do."

My heart skips three beats. "So who took it?"

"Crayvon." She points up the street. "He lives in that yellow house with the red car in the driveway."

"How do you know Crayvon took it?"

"Because I saw them sneaking into Kennedy's backyard like you did a minute ago."

"Them who?"

"Graylin and Crayvon."

"If both of them went back there, how do you know Crayvon was the one who took it?"

"I just do."

"Do you remember which day it was?"

"I think it was Wednesday. Graylin got arrested on Friday."

"Did you tell anybody?"

"Nope. I didn't want to get them in trouble. Nobody likes Kennedy. She acts like that's her real hair, but it's not. It's just a three-hundred-dollar weave that looks like real hair."

Kennedy's weave is not what I want to know about. "What time of day was it?"

"Hmmm," Taisha puts a finger to her chin. "Around five o'clock maybe. It wasn't dark yet."

"Do you know how long they were back there?"

"About five minutes. They both ran out laughing."

"Was Kennedy at home?"

"I don't know."

I can't believe I've stumbled upon this witness. I'm so stunned my mind goes blank.

"I hope you have some more questions for me. Otherwise, you're not that good of an investigator."

I laugh. "Well, help me out. What other questions should I be asking you?"

Taisha smiles deviously. "You should ask me if I saw anybody else go back into Kennedy's backyard that same day after Crayvon and Graylin came out."

"Did you?"

"Yep?"

"Who?"

"Crayvon. And this time, Graylin wasn't with him. I bet you anything Crayvon took that picture and is trying to pin it on Graylin. Graylin's nice. He always says hi to me. Crayvon's the one who would do something like that. Not Graylin."

"Why would you say that?"

"Because he stuck his hand underneath Nedra Johnson's dress in Sunday school class. He lied and said he didn't do it. But I saw him with my own eyes."

"Tai, who are you talking to out there?" A woman opens the screen door and steps onto the porch.

"Hi, my name is Mei." I'm worried that this woman won't like the idea of a stranger talking to her daughter. "I'm an investigator hired by Graylin Alexander's attorneys. He's the boy—"

"I know who he is. His family goes to my church. It's a shame what they're doing to that child."

"I didn't get your name," I say.

"Betty. Betty Taylor. And I guess you've met my daughter Taisha. She's quite a little talker."

"Yes, she is. She gave me some information that could be very important to Graylin's defense."

"Oh, did she?" Betty says with raised eyebrows.

"Tai, why don't you go inside and wash your hands? We'll be eating in a minute."

Betty waits until Taisha is inside and motions me back down the walkway. I assume to make sure Taisha doesn't overhear us.

"I don't know what Taisha told you, but whatever she said, I'd take it with a grain of salt. She's my foster daughter. A very troubled kid. Half of what comes out of her mouth is pure fantasy. I've had dozens of foster children over the years, but I've never had one who lies as much as this one."

"She told me she saw Crayvon sneaking into Kennedy's back-yard a couple of days before Graylin was arrested." I decide not to mention the part about Graylin going in with him earlier. "Did she tell you that?"

"No, and I wouldn't put any stock in it. She lies the way you and I breathe. She can't help it. I think it's a cry for attention."

I've interviewed tons of people. Liars often display red flags, like not making eye contact, excessive blinking or shifting their eyes to the left or right. I picked up no such flags from Taisha.

"I think I'd sense it if Taisha wasn't telling me the truth," I say, unwilling to disregard the goldmine of information she's given me.

"Oh, no you wouldn't." Betty rests a hand on her hip and smiles. "When it comes to telling lies, Taisha is very, very good at it."

# CHAPTER 39

## *Angela*

Graylin's preliminary hearing starts in fifty-two minutes. Jenny, Graylin and I march into the Criminal Courts Building in downtown Los Angeles like soldiers heading off to war. In a way, we are.

We've filed a motion to suppress Graylin's interrogation by police and the cell phone picture too. If things don't go our way and the case proceeds to trial, all isn't lost thanks to Mei. The information she got from Taisha about Crayvon going into Kennedy's backyard and putting his hand underneath a girl's dress at church lifted our spirits.

Of course, the information about Graylin also being in Kennedy's backyard does concern us. We haven't discussed it with him yet for fear of distracting him. We need Graylin one hundred percent focused on the prelim.

"You ready to testify," Jenny asks as we all clear the metal detectors.

"Yep," Graylin says, smiling. He's dressed in one of his church suits with a light-blue tie. His hair has been freshly cut and he's even wearing a lemony-smelling cologne. So much of it, in fact, that it stings my nose.

Jenny squeezes his shoulder. "Don't forget that Angela's going to lead you every step of the way. Just like we practiced."

"I know," Graylin says, showing not a lick of nervousness. "I told you, I got this."

I press the elevator button. "And remember that the prosecutor is going to be very nice when she asks you questions," I remind him. "But she's not on your side. So listen very carefully to her questions before you answer."

"Don't worry, Ms. Angela. I watched three episodes of *Law & Order* last night. I know how prosecutors try to trick people. She's not going to trip me up. I'm too smart for that."

As we step off the elevator onto the fifth floor, Graylin clutches my arm with the desperation of a drowning swimmer.

"What's the matter?" I say.

His face is ashen and his lips are quivering. I follow his gaze and see two uniformed police officers sitting on a bench down the hallway.

Graylin's grasp on my arm tightens even more. "Those are the cops who arrested me!"

He darts behind my back, almost tripping me. I try to pull my arm free, but Graylin won't let go.

"Calm down," Jenny says. "They can't do anything to you."

"Are they going to be in the courtroom looking at me when I testify?" he whimpers.

"No," Jenny assures him. "They'll have to wait outside."

The tension doesn't leave Graylin's face. He's been upbeat since getting out on bail. The obnoxious teenager who disrupted the fitness hearing instantly morphed back into the sweet kid I know and love.

Jenny and I surround him, blocking his view of the cops as we walk past them.

Dre and Gus are already seated on the back row of the gallery. I'm glad to see that the Carlyles aren't here.

Graylin stops to give his worried father a hug. Dre hugs him too. Graylin's relationship with Gus has definitely been fractured. I can see the weight of Gus' fear for his son written all over his face. I swear he's aged a few years since Graylin's arrest.

We take a seat at the defense table with Graylin sitting between us.

The prosecutor walks in, sets her files down on the table, then comes over to introduce herself. Lorelei Sullivan is short with fiery-red hair and a friendly smile. She conveys the kind of self-assurance that would make you automatically gravitate toward her at a cocktail party.

A rear door opens and Judge Calvin Fuller takes the bench. "I understand we're here for a preliminary hearing," the judge says after we've stated our appearances for the record.

He's a good draw for us. A fiftyish, South Central native and Hastings Law School grad, he's smart, socially conscious and knows from experience that all cops aren't good cops. He's tall with salt-and-pepper hair and a distinctive goatee.

"Call your first witness, Ms. Sullivan," Judge Fuller says.

The prosecution's first witness is L.A.P.D. Officer Alan Chin. The bailiff steps outside and escorts Chin into the courtroom. Sullivan asks a handful of questions about his background, then moves on to Graylin's arrest.

"When you showed up at Marcus Preparatory Academy on May tenth, what was your understanding of the reason the police were called?"

"The principal received a report that the defendant had a naked picture of another student, Kennedy Carlyle, on his phone. The report also said that the defendant threatened to post the picture all over the Internet to embarrass the girl."

"What happened when you arrived at the school?"

"The defendant was waiting for us in the principal's office. We asked him if he wanted to speak to us and he agreed, so we took him into the principal's conference room."

Graylin is squirming like a worm, whispering to us that the cop is lying on him. Jenny is trying to calm him down so I can concentrate on taking notes for my cross.

"Did you identify yourself as a police officer?" Sullivan asks.

"Yes."

"Was anyone else with you?"

"Yes, my partner, Officer Fenton."

"What happened once you went into the conference room?"

"I asked him if he had a naked picture of Kennedy Carlyle on his phone and he lied and said no."

"Did you ask him if you could look at his phone?"

"Yes. He lied again and said it was in his locker, but then the phone started ringing."

"Then what happened?"

"I asked him if I could see his phone and he said okay. So he handed it to my partner. Fenton didn't see anything on it, but when I checked his deleted pictures, I found it."

"Could you describe the picture?"

"It appeared to be a young girl in a bedroom. She was standing and was completely naked."

"Did you later confirm the identity of the girl in the picture?"

"Yes, Kennedy Carlyle, a classmate of the defendant."

"When the defendant voluntarily entered the conference room to speak with you, was he under arrest?"

"No."

"So he was free to leave at any time?"

"Of course."

"At any time during your meeting with the defendant, did you tell him that he couldn't leave the room?"

"No. And he never once asked to leave."

"And did you force him to hand over his phone?"

"No. He willingly gave it to us."

"And how long did the interview last?"

"Fifteen, twenty minutes, tops."

"No further questions," Sullivan says.

I'm standing even before the judge gives me the go-ahead.

"Officer Chin, since you knew that you were being called to Marcus Prep because a student allegedly had a naked picture on his phone, did you obtain a search warrant for my client's phone before showing up at the school?"

"No."

"Did you read my client his Miranda rights before commencing your interrogation?"

"No. He wasn't under arrest. We were just talking to him."

"Did you examine the so-called report that my client had a naked picture on his phone?"

He shrugs. "Yeah. The principal showed the note to me."

"Was that note signed by anyone?"

"No."

"And you felt you had probable cause to interrogate my client based on a simple anonymous note?"

"It wasn't an interrogation. Anyway, we didn't need probable cause since your client agreed to talk to us."

"Isn't it correct that you ordered my client into the conference room?"

"No. We asked him if he wanted to talk to us and he agreed."

"What were your exact words?"

Officer Chin repositions himself in the chair. "It was something like, *Would you like to talk with us?* And he said, *Okay.*"

I hear the muffled voice of Graylin behind me and I'm praying Jenny can quiet him down.

"Didn't Graylin tell you that his father told him not to talk to the police without his permission?"

"I think he may have mentioned that."

"How many times?"

"At least once."

"Wasn't it more like four or five times?"

"No, I don't think it was that many."

"So why did you continue to question him after he told you that his father told him not to speak to the police without his permission?"

"We're only required to suspend questioning if someone asks for an attorney and he didn't do that. And, like I said, it wasn't like he was under arrest or anything. If he didn't want to talk to us, he could've left."

"So you think a fourteen-year-old boy locked in a conference room with two police officers would think he could just get up and walk out?"

"Well, he could."

"Was he also free to leave school grounds anytime he felt like it?"

"Objection, calls for speculation," Sullivan says.

Judge Fuller takes two beats before responding. "Overruled. The witness can answer."

Chin is bright enough to follow Sullivan's lead and avoid speculating. "I don't know the school's rules. I only know that the defendant was free to leave the conference room."

"Did you pound the table with your fist and say, *Give me the damn phone*?"

"I asked for the phone. I don't recall pounding the table."

Graylin's voice disrupts my focus. "But he's lying on me, Ms. Jenny!"

"Isn't it correct that you demanded that my client give you his password?"

"No, we didn't demand anything."

"Did Graylin type in his password?"

"I don't remember."

"I have no further questions."

As soon as I return to the defense table, Graylin grabs my arm. "He's lying, Ms. Angela," he says, near tears. "He made me give him the phone! I didn't know I could leave!"

"I know. I need you to calm down. Getting upset won't help your case. The judge knows he's lying." *At least I hope he does.*

Sullivan doesn't do a redirect, so Officer Chin is dismissed. The bailiff retrieves Officer Fenton from the hallway. Sullivan only asks him enough questions to back up Officer Chin's statements, then hands him over to me.

"Officer Fenton, didn't my client repeatedly say that his father had instructed him not to talk to the police without his permission?"

"Yes, he did mention that."

"How many times?"

"I'm not quite sure."

"At least three?"

"Probably."

"At least four times?"

"Maybe."

"So if your partner testified that it was only one time, you would disagree with that, correct?"

His shoulders hunch and his eyes dart toward the prosecutor. "It's hard to remember the exact number."

"How close were you sitting to my client while you were interrogating him?"

"I was sitting next to him."

"And your chair was turned sideways so you were facing the side of his body, correct?"

"Yes."

"And your knee was touching his leg, correct?

Officer Fenton stutters. "I-I don't remember."

"You don't remember touching his leg?"

"Well, I may have."

"Did Officer Chin pound the table with his fist during the interrogation of Graylin?"

"He might have."

"He might have or he did?"

"Yeah, I guess he did."

"Do you think Graylin was intimidated by that?"

Sullivan jumps in before he can answer. "Objection, calls for speculation."

"Sustained," the judge says.

"Did Graylin look scared when Officer Chin pounded the table?"

"Yeah, a little. I guess."

"Didn't he start crying?"

Fenton shrugs again. "Yeah, after we found out he was lying about having his phone with him."

"And didn't he even wet his pants?"

"Yeah, but we weren't aware of that until we put him in the squad car."

"When Officer Chin pounded the table with his fist, did he say to Graylin, *Give me the damn phone*?"

"Yeah, something like that."

"And you typed in Graylin's password, not him, correct?"

"Yeah, but he gave it to us."

"I have no further questions, Your Honor."

Sullivan doesn't do a redirect and tells the judge she has no further witnesses.

Judge Fuller turns to me. "Call your first witness."

I say a quick prayer and return to my feet. "The defense calls Graylin Alexander."

# CHAPTER 40

## *Angela*

As Graylin approaches the witness stand, I pray he sticks to our script. It's always risky to have a defendant testify at the prelim because his statements can be used against him at trial. We have an order, however, limiting Graylin's testimony to the circumstances of his interrogation. I plan to get him on and off the stand as quickly as possible.

Graylin looks like a miniature country preacher sitting in the witness box. His tightly clasped hands highlight his nervousness.

"Did your teacher take you to the principal's office on May tenth?" I begin.

"Yes, ma'am."

"Did two police officers come into the office while you were there?"

"Yes."

"What did they say to you?"

"The Asian one, Officer Chin, made me go into the principal's conference room."

"Did you think you could disobey his order?"

Sullivan is on her feet. "Objection to the use of the word *order*."

The judge grunts. "Sustained."

I rephrase my question. "When Officer Chin took you into the principal's conference room, did you think you could refuse to go?"

"No, ma'am. I had to do what the police officer told me to do. Just like I have to obey my teachers."

"Did the police officers tell you that you didn't have to go into the principal's office if you didn't want to?"

"No."

"Did they close the door when you went into the principal's office?"

"Yes."

"Did you think you could leave?"

"No. I had to stay there until they said I could go. I thought I was under arrest."

"When they started asking you questions, did you tell them you didn't want to talk to them?"

"Yes. I kept telling them that my dad told me not to speak to the police without his permission. But they ignored what I was saying and kept asking me questions."

"How many times did you tell them that your dad told you not to speak to the police without his permission?"

"A lot."

That wasn't the answer we had rehearsed.

"Do you remember how many times?"

There's a flash of recognition in his eyes as he appears to recall our prep session. "At least four or five times."

"So when Officer Chin testified that it was only once, that wasn't the truth?"

"No, it wasn't. He said a lot of things that weren't true like—"

I hold up my hand. We instructed Graylin to follow my lead and not jump ahead of me. We also told him that if I raise my hand, that means he isn't following my instructions.

Graylin lowers his head and tucks in his chin. I smile at him, so he's not discouraged by my rebuke.

"When the police officers asked you for your phone, did you think you could refuse to give it to them?"

"No, ma'am. That's why I told them it was in my locker because I didn't want to give it to them. But when it started ringing, Officer Chin pounded the table with his fist and said, *Give me the damn phone.*"

"How did you feel when Officer Chin pounded the table with his fist and said, *Give me the damn phone?*"

"I was scared. I knew I had to do what he said."

"Where were the two officers sitting?"

"Officer Chin was sitting on the other side of the table, but Officer Fenton was sitting on my left, really close to me. He was facing me and his knee was bumping my thigh."

"How did that make you feel?"

"Scared."

"I have no further questions."

Sullivan walks over to the witness box and stands even closer to Graylin than I was.

"Good afternoon, Graylin, my name is Lorelei Sullivan and I'm the prosecutor. I only have a few questions for you. Do you watch legal shows on TV?"

"Yes."

"Have you ever seen *Law & Order?*"

"Yes."

"What about *Boston Legal?*"

"Yes. But *The First 48* is my favorite."

*Jesus.* He's letting his guard down already.

"So you're familiar with Miranda rights, correct?"

"Yes. That's when you have the right to remain silent."

My stomach flips. We instructed Graylin to answer yes or no to Sullivan's questions whenever possible. Nothing more.

"That's right. Did you ever tell the officers that you didn't want to talk to them?"

"Um, yes. But not in those exact words. I told them that my dad told me not to speak to the police without his permission. So that's the same thing."

Sullivan wasn't expecting that response. She moves on.

"When Officer Chin asked for your phone, what did you think would happen if you didn't give it to him?"

Jenny glances over at me. We're both holding our breath.

"That he would arrest me."

"Okay, so then you didn't think you were already under arrest when you were in the principal's conference room, correct?"

Graylin squints and does exactly what we told him to do if a question confused him. He pauses and thinks about his response before speaking.

"No, ma'am, that's not correct. He didn't tell me I was under arrest yet, but I knew I couldn't leave the room, so that's the same thing as being under arrest."

"But you said you thought the officers would arrest you if you didn't give them your phone. So it doesn't sound like you thought you were under arrest yet."

Graylin sits taller in the chair. "What I meant to say is that I thought they would take me to jail. I knew I was already under arrest since they had me locked up in the conference room with them."

*You go, boy!* Jenny and I trade a glance that's the equivalent of a high-five.

Sullivan rolls her eyes and plows ahead.

"When you first sat down to talk to the two officers, you wanted to explain your side of the story so you wouldn't get in trouble, right?"

Graylin pauses. "Um, yes."

I wince.

"But not until after I spoke to my dad," Graylin quickly adds.

"Now, didn't you lie to the police about having a naked picture—"

Like twin Jack in the boxes, Jenny and I shoot to our feet, shouting in unison, "Objection!"

"That question is outside the scope of our motion to suppress," I say. "The prosecutor is violating the court's instruction."

Judge Fuller gives Sullivan a chiding look. "Sustained. Don't test me, counselor." Then he turns to the defense table. "I only need objections from one of you at a time."

Sullivan steps even closer to Graylin and rests her forearm on the corner of the witness box. "You're a good student, aren't you, Graylin?"

"Yes, I get mostly A's."

"Would you say that you're mature for your age?"

Graylin squints. "Um, everybody says I'm big for my age. Is that what you mean?"

I don't like the path Sullivan is heading down.

"Not exactly. Do you consider yourself to be very responsible?"

"Yes."

"Give me some examples of how you're responsible."

I tap my fingers on the desk. We didn't prep Graylin for this line of questioning. I get to my feet.

"Your Honor, I object to the question as beyond the scope of our motion."

Sullivan doesn't wait for the judge's response. "I disagree. The defendant's maturity level is directly relevant to whether his actions were voluntary."

"Overruled," the judge says.

Sullivan turns back to Graylin. "Can you give me some examples of how you're mature?"

"Um," Graylin looks out at me, but I can't help him. "Um, I do my chores and my homework without being told. I babysit my little cousin, Keesha." He stops and looks up at the ceiling. "I go with my granny to the grocery store and help her with the shopping. I also put a schedule on her calendar so she knows when to take her blood pressure and thyroid pills. Stuff like that."

"Wow, that's wonderful," Sullivan says, exaggerating her praise. "When you went into the conference room with Officers Chin and Fenton, did they lock the door?"

Graylin pauses. "I don't know if they locked it, but they closed it."

"Did the officers ever tell you that you couldn't leave the room?"

"No. But the way police are always shooting innocent black men, I knew I had to do everything they told me to do, which means I couldn't leave the room. And I had to give them my phone when they asked for it."

I can't help but smile. He's not supposed to go off script, but that little zinger was fine with me.

Sullivan frowns and walks back over to the prosecution table to look at her notes. After a few seconds, she says, "No further questions."

Graylin rushes off the stand and returns to his seat. "Did I do good, Ms. Angela?"

"You did great. The best witness I've ever had. And I mean it."

"Ms. Evans, call your next witness," the judge says.

"That's it, Your Honor. I have no further witnesses."

"Let's take a ten-minute break," Judge Fuller says. "When we return, I'll hear brief oral arguments, then give you my decision."

# CHAPTER **41**

## *Angela*

As we wait to begin oral arguments, I now regret eating breakfast this morning, something I never do before an important court appearance. There's a strong possibility my scrambled eggs could end up splattered on the courtroom floor.

"You did great," Jenny tells me. "You got Fenton to contradict his partner more than once. That has to weigh heavily with the judge."

"We'll see."

The judge only listens to our arguments for about five minutes before tapping his gavel. "Okay, counsel, I've heard enough. I'm ready to rule. You may be seated."

"The courts are clear," Judge Fuller begins, "that when a minor being questioned by police asks for a parent, that does not mean the minor has invoked his or her constitutional right to remain silent."

My stomach drops. Graylin looks over at me, his forehead etched with deep lines of confusion.

"Despite repeating that his father told him not to talk to the police without his permission, the defendant continued talking to them anyway, and even turned over his phone to them. He's a bright, mature young man, as evidenced by the way he helps his grandmother and his strong grades. So on the issue of whether he acted voluntarily in speaking with police, I must side with the prosecution.

"I also don't find that the circumstances of the interrogation were sufficiently coercive to rise to the level of a custodial interrogation. The police did nothing to prevent the defendant from leaving the room. It was a relatively short interrogation and he wasn't deprived of sleep or food.

"As such, defense counsel's motion to suppress the defendant's statements, his phone and any evidence retrieved from the phone is denied. I also find that the prosecution has met its burden of demonstrating probable cause as to each of the charges filed against the defendant."

The judge rises and disappears into his chambers.

Graylin's lips are quivering as a tear rolls down his left cheek. "The police lied on me, Ms. Angela. I didn't want to talk to them. They made me do it!"

"I know."

We walk toward the back of the courtroom, where Graylin collapses into his father's arms.

# CHAPTER 42

## *Angela*

With the trial date looming, it's time for us to focus on our star witness.

When we arrive at Crayvon's home, Mrs. Little greets us warmly and shows us into the dining room.

"Crayvon'll be here in a minute. He went to Home Depot with my sister. I'll be right back with some coffee."

"I don't think she's going to be so nice to us once she realizes we're here to throw her son under the bus," Jenny whispers.

"If Crayvon took that picture and set up Graylin, he deserves to be under a bus."

Mrs. Little sets a plate with several slices of pound cake in the middle of the table, then returns with cream, sugar and three mugs of coffee.

"I've been praying every night for Graylin and his family," Mrs. Little says. "It's not right what they're doing to him. They're just kids. I tell Crayvon all the time, he better not be doing that sexting stuff."

A tall, skinny kid charges through the front door and into the dining room, almost out of breath. He immediately reaches for a piece of cake, but his mother slaps his hand.

"Boy, where are your manners? Say hello, then go wash your hands."

After quick introductions, Crayvon dashes out and returns in seconds. He sits on one side of the table with his mother. Jenny and I are on the other.

Jenny is chomping on Mrs. Little's pound cake as if it's a foreign delicacy. "Mrs. Little, this is the best pound cake I've ever tasted. You must give me the recipe."

"It's the coconut and pineapple that make the difference," she says proudly. "Sorry, though. It's a family secret."

We know we have to ease into our questioning, so we take it slow, asking a series of softball questions about Crayvon's school activities and his friendship with Graylin. Every few seconds, Mrs. Little interrupts.

"Those boys are closer than two peas in a pod. I almost feel like he's my son. You know, his mother isn't around, right?"

We nod and continue with our questions.

"Do you know Taisha Mitchell?" Jenny asks.

Crayvon takes a bite of pound cake. "Yeah. She lives up the street. She's a foster kid. She's weird."

"Boy, don't talk with your mouth full," his mother scolds him. "And don't be calling that child weird. You're blessed that you have a family."

"Tell us what you know about her," Jenny says.

"Nothing really. She attends my church, but she doesn't go to our school."

"Is she friends with Kennedy?"

"She used to be, but not anymore. Now LaShay is Kennedy's best friend."

"What do you know about LaShay?"

"She's in my algebra and English classes. She's kinda quiet."

Jenny reaches for her second piece of pound cake.

"What about Kennedy? Are you friends with her?" I ask.

"Nope."

"Do you have any idea who might've taken that picture of her?"

"Nope."

"Right before your second-period class, you told Graylin you had to go to the administration office. Why?"

"My first-period teacher, Mrs. Bosley, asked me to drop off some papers for her."

I make a note for Mei to confirm that with his teacher.

I inhale, knowing that my next series of questions are likely to spark a change in demeanor from both Crayvon and Mrs. Little. Jenny senses where I'm about to go and gives me an out.

"Mrs. Little, could I bother you for some more coffee?"

"Of course." She stands up and retrieves Jenny's mug. "It'll only take a minute or so. Since I'm the only one who drinks coffee, I bought one of those single-cup coffeemakers."

I wink at Jenny. She intentionally guzzled down her coffee so Mrs. Little would have to go get her a refill.

When Mrs. Little leaves the room, I lower my voice a bit, praying she can't hear us from the kitchen. "Taisha says she saw you and Graylin going into Kennedy's backyard a couple of days before Graylin was arrested. Is that true?"

Crayvon stops chewing and his eyes dart toward the kitchen. He seems as concerned about his mother overhearing us as we are.

"Um, well, we went back there, but we didn't do anything."

Mrs. Little must have dog ears. She flies back into the room, no mug in hand. "Wait a minute. When were you in the Carlyles' backyard?"

"Um, I don't remember. But Graylin went with me."

"What were you guys doing back there?" I ask.

"Nothing. We were just messing around. We snuck in there and ran right back out."

Mrs. Little sits back down next to her son. Her lips are on the edge of a frown.

"Taisha told us you two were back there about five minutes," I say.

"Yeah. We were looking around. Kennedy's backyard is huge. They have a big waterfall."

Mrs. Little's arms are folded now and she's giving her son a look to kill.

I know we're going to get that same look in about two seconds.

"Taisha said that after Graylin left, you came back a little later by yourself and went back there again."

Crayvon jumps to his feet. "No, I—"

Before he can finish, Mrs. Little blows a fuse. "Oh, hell naw!" She pushes her chair back, plants her hands flat on the table and leans in. "You're not going to pin this on my baby!"

I hold up my palms. "We're just following up on what Taisha told our investigator. We—"

"I know exactly what you're trying to do." Her smooth face is now wrinkled with rage. "You are *not* going to make my child Graylin's scapegoat. Get out of my house!"

Jenny reaches for another piece of pound cake, but Mrs. Little snatches the plate away.

"I said get out. Now!"

# CHAPTER 43

## *Angela*

Two days after getting thrown out of Crayvon's house, we decide it's finally time to talk to Graylin about being in Kennedy's backyard.

I park in front of Graylin's apartment complex as Jenny pulls up behind me.

"Hey," Jenny says, getting out of her car. "I picked up some donuts."

"I'm surprised you didn't go back to Crayvon's house and ask for some more of that pound cake."

Jenny laughs. "I would have if I thought I had a chance of getting another piece."

Graylin greets both of us with hugs and wastes no time digging into the donuts.

"Is someone here with you?" Jenny asks. Graylin is supposed to be under twenty-four-hour supervision.

"Yep. My granny's in her bedroom watching *The Haves and the Have Nots*. When that show comes on nobody can bother her."

Being in the same house with Graylin isn't proper supervision. He's wearing an ankle monitor, but even so, he could've sneaked out and returned without his grandmother ever knowing. I plan to talk to Gus about this.

"Okay," Jenny begins, as we settle into the living room, "we want to talk to you about some new information we discovered."

Hope floods Graylin's face. "You found out who sent me the picture?"

"No, not yet," Jenny says. "We have some questions to ask you and you need to be honest with us."

Graylin bites into a donut and a blob of strawberry jelly dribbles onto his white T-shirt. "Okay."

We've agreed that Jenny will take the lead on questioning Graylin so that I can pay closer attention to his demeanor. We have to be certain he's telling us the truth.

"Do you know Taisha Mitchell?" Jenny asks.

He stops to think. "Yeah. She lives on Crayvon's street with a foster family. She goes to my church."

"Our investigator interviewed her and she said she saw you and Crayvon going into Kennedy's backyard a few days before you got arrested. Is that true?"

Graylin almost chokes on his donut. "Um, yeah."

"Why didn't you tell us that?"

He lowers his head. "You didn't ask me, Ms. Jenny. And if I'd told you I'd gone back there, you would've thought I'd taken that picture of her."

"Did you take the picture?" she asks.

His head shoots back up. "No ma'am! I swear! You have to believe me. We were only playing around. They have a huge waterfall. We weren't even back there that long. Crayvon's the one who likes her, not me."

"Crayvon likes Kennedy?"

"Yeah."

"You didn't tell us that either."

"You didn't ask me."

That's the problem with a child client. They often don't understand the relevance of certain information.

"Do you remember when you went back there?"

"Yes, it was on Tuesday, that same week that I got arrested."

"How do you remember that?"

"Because we have Math Club meetings after school on Tuesdays and sometimes I go to Crayvon's house afterward to help him with his algebra."

"After you two came out of Kennedy's backyard," Jenny continues, "what did you do?"

"I went home."

"What time did you go home?"

"I don't remember. But I'm sure it wasn't dark yet because I'm not allowed to ride the bus at night."

"Did you take any pictures while you were back there?"

"No, Ms. Jenny. You have to believe me. And Crayvon didn't take any pictures either."

"Taisha said she saw Crayvon go back into Kennedy's backyard by himself a few minutes after you left."

Graylin shrugs. "I wouldn't know. I went home."

It takes a couple of seconds for his brain to process the implication of Jenny's statement. And when he does, outrage crawls across his face like an ugly rash.

"I knew it! Crayvon took that picture! He set me up!"

"We don't know that for sure," Jenny says. "We spoke to him too. He says he didn't take it."

Graylin didn't seem to hear Jenny's words. "I was wondering why he hasn't called or come by to see me since I've been out. That's why! Because he set me up!"

"Calm down, Graylin," I say. "We don't know that for sure."

"I do! I thought he was my best friend." He starts to cry. "How could he do this to me? You have to tell the police it was Crayvon and not me!"

# CHAPTER 44

## *Angela*

Graylin's trial is less than a month away. Now that we have a plausible suspect to point the finger at—Crayvon—our energy level is off the charts.

Jenny and I are headed into the apartment building of LaShay Baker, Kennedy's best friend. When we called to set up the interview, the girl's grandmother was more than receptive.

Naomi Baker opens the front door before we can even knock.

"Get on in here and give me a hug!" she says, throwing her arms wide open.

Mrs. Baker is a tall, bulky woman with a gracious smile who speaks in a booming female baritone.

She squeezes me so hard I gasp for air. When she gives Jenny the same treatment, I almost burst out laughing.

We're shown into a living room that's a throwback to the 1970s. There's beige shag carpeting and her antique couch has plastic slipcovers.

"I'm so proud of you girls. Graylin's a good boy and I'm glad he has you two fighting for him."

"So you know Graylin?" Jenny asks, still massaging her ribcage.

"No, but LaShay told me all about him. And the Holy Spirit tells me things. He's a good boy. I can feel it."

Jenny throws me a bewildered glance. She's wondering if Mrs. Baker is playing with a full deck.

"Mrs. Baker," I begin, "we wanted to talk with LaShay about—"

"Everybody calls me Mama Baker," the woman says. "So you girls should call me that too. I made some coffee." She points to a white decanter sitting on the coffee table. "Let me go get the food I prepared."

Mama Baker returns carrying a silver platter with finger sandwiches and chocolate cake cut into neat triangles. Jenny eyes the food like she just ended a ten-day fast. She reaches for the cake first and immediately starts gushing.

"This cake is absolutely amazing!"

"Is LaShay here?" I ask as Jenny chows down. Cake must be her thing. I'm jealous that she can eat like a pig and remain as thin as a straw.

"Oh, I'm sorry. I guess y'all didn't come here to chit-chat with me." She yells down the hallway. "LaShay! Come in here, baby!"

A petite girl wearing cornrows appears in the entryway.

Mama Baker pats the couch next to her. "Graylin's attorneys wanna talk to you, baby."

LaShay perches herself on the edge of the couch, across from us. She rests her hands in her lap, which is also where she keeps her gaze.

I take the lead since Jenny is too busy munching. "We understand that you're friends with Kennedy Carlyle."

The girl nods. "Yes. She's my best friend."

"Then you know about the picture that was taken of her?"

LaShay nods again.

"Can you think of anybody who might've wanted to hurt Kennedy by taking that picture."

"Nope."

"Did Kennedy ever say she knew who took it?"

"Yeah. She said Graylin took it."

"Do you know why she thinks that?"

"Because he had it on his phone and because that's what everybody is saying at school."

"Do you know Crayvon Little?"

"Yes."

"Did Crayvon like Kennedy?"

"Yep, he told me he wanted her to be his girlfriend. But she can't stand him because he's always making jokes about her."

Jenny takes a break from her orgasm over the cake to ask a question. "When did he do that?"

"All the time. He's always trying to embarrass her."

"Can you give us an example of something he did to embarrass her?" I ask.

"One time, in the cafeteria in front of everybody, he called her stuck-up and said her breasts were flatter than pancakes. Everybody laughed. It really hurt Kennedy's feelings."

Mama Baker shakes her head. "These kids today are a mess with all this bullying stuff."

For the next thirty minutes or so we listen to LaShay's depiction of middle school life.

"Did Kennedy ever report Crayvon to a teacher or anyone else at school?" I ask.

"Nope. She was too afraid."

"Afraid of what?"

"If she reported him and he got in trouble, he might start teasing her more."

"Did Kennedy ever tell you she saw Crayvon or Graylin in her backyard before?"

"No."

Jenny asks a few more questions, then gives me a look that says she's all out. I'm about to announce that we're done when another question comes to mind.

"Do you know if Kennedy has started counseling yet?"

"Nope," LaShay says.

"Why not?"

"Because her daddy doesn't believe in it. He says he doesn't like telling strangers their business."

"You don't take your problems to man," Mama Baker says. "You take them to Jesus."

With that, we begin packing up to leave. Mama Baker asks if we'd like to take some cake to go. Jenny doesn't even let the woman get the words out before saying yes.

Mama Baker leaves the room and returns carrying two Ziploc bags with the cake wrapped in foil inside.

"Would you girls mind if I lay hands on you?" Mama Baker asks, moving in without waiting for our consent.

Jenny's eyes blaze with uncertainty. She has no idea what that means.

"That's fine," I say. Jenny remains mum, clutching her cake.

Mama Baker stands facing us. She grips the front of our heads, curling the heel of her large hands underneath our foreheads, and starts to pray.

"Father, I ask you today to bless these two young women with the power to bring justice where justice is long overdue. Give them all your power, Father, to get little Graylin out of this mess. Help these girls convince that jury that if the glove don't fit, they must acquit."

I glance over at Jenny, who has one eye open. She looks petrified. Mama Baker goes on for what seems like another five minutes.

"That I ask of you in Jesus' name. Amen! Hallelujah!" She squeezes both our heads then gently pushes us, sending us stumbling backward a step or two.

"Thank you so much," I say.

"You're welcome, baby. Now give Mama Baker another hug."

She pulls me into her arms, then turns to Jenny, who crosses her eyes at me over Mama Baker's shoulder.

"What was that head-grabbing thing?" Jenny says as we're walking to our cars. "I should've told her I'm Jewish."

"I'm glad you didn't," I say laughing. "She might've given you an extra special prayer and we might still be there."

# CHAPTER 45

## Angela

The days zip by and we're finally seated in the courtroom of Judge Erik Lipscomb about to start day one of Graylin's trial. He takes the bench promptly at nine and gets things rolling.

Sullivan's opening statement is brief and to the point. She spends way too much time on reasonable doubt and little time on what she's going to prove. Her final appeal tells me she senses that we're banking on jury nullification.

"In deciding this case, I ask that you put your personal feelings aside and focus on the law," she urges the jury. "You may not like the fact that minors are being prosecuted for possession of child pornography, but what the defendant did is wrong and it shouldn't be tolerated, regardless of whether he's an adult sex offender or a fourteen-year-old child predator. There's a young girl whose naked picture has been circulated all over the Internet. She deserves justice. And the only way to give her justice is to listen to all the evidence, apply the law and find the defendant guilty as charged on all counts."

I take a quick sip of water before standing up. I round the defense table and face the jury.

"Contrary to what you just heard from the prosecutor," I begin, "this case is not about a child predator or about protecting children. This is a case about a kid being a kid. My client, Graylin Alexander," I turn to face him, "received a picture via a popular social media app called Snapchat. If you have teenage kids, there's a good chance they have a Snapchat account. Graylin opened a Snapchat message and, to his surprise, someone had sent him a naked picture. A naked picture of one of his classmates.

"What did he do? What any fourteen-year-old might do. He saved the picture to his cell phone. He didn't show the picture to anyone. He didn't send the picture to anyone. He didn't post it on social media. He simply took a screenshot of it. That's it. That's why he's here. Graylin Alexander—an A student who's active in his church, who's loved and respected by his teachers and classmates, who's never had any contact with the criminal justice system—took a screenshot of a picture someone sent him. That's why the prosecutor charged him with a number of sex-related crimes that will change his life forever."

I gently shake my head to show my dismay.

"I want you to listen very carefully to every witness and follow the law. But I also want you to use your common sense. If what you hear doesn't seem right, then maybe it isn't."

I pause. This is as close as I can get to asking for jury nullification. I'll hit it harder in my closing. I go on for another ten minutes before wrapping up.

"Graylin Alexander is a kid," I finally say. "He did something any kid—even your kid—might do in the same situation. He expressed his adolescent curiosity. He's not a criminal. Don't punish this kid for simply being a kid."

I take a few seconds to look into the eyes of as many jurors as I can, then walk back to my seat.

"You did good, Ms. Angela!" Graylin reaches over and gives me a hug as soon as I sit down. He's already forgotten my admonition about not showing emotion in front of the jury.

I assumed Sullivan's first witness would be one of the cops. Instead, she calls Simone Carlyle to the stand. Kennedy is in the courtroom to witness her mother's testimony. This is the first time I've had a chance to see the girl in person. She looks small and frail sitting next to her father. All this time, my focus has been on Graylin, not Kennedy, the victim. And today, my heart goes out to her.

Mrs. Carlyle testifies along the same lines as she did during the detention hearing, her testimony intended to elicit sympathy for her daughter.

"What impact has this tragic invasion of privacy had on your daughter?" Sullivan asks.

"My baby hasn't been the same since," Simone Carlyle says with a sniffle. She wipes away a non-existent tear. "Teenagers are so sensitive. What that boy did to my baby was the worst kind of crime."

"Objection," I say. "The witness has no evidence that my client committed any crime."

"Sustained," declares the judge.

Every time she utters the words *my baby*, Mrs. Carlyle glances out at Kennedy and so does the jury. If Sullivan wants the jurors to feel sorry for the girl, Mrs. Carlyle's performance is getting the job done.

On cross, I know I have to be delicate with her or the jury could turn on me. I have only one area to pursue.

"Mrs. Carlyle, is Kennedy seeing a therapist?"

Sullivan cuts in. "Objection, Your Honor. This line of questioning is irrelevant and an invasion of the victim's privacy."

"I don't plan to inquire about the specifics of her therapy," I protest. "My question goes directly to whether the victim has suffered the degree of emotional distress that her mother claims."

"This isn't a civil case," Sullivan counters. "The state doesn't have to prove the victim suffered emotional distress."

The judge mulls over our objections. "I'll allow it. Overruled."

Mrs. Carlyle gawks at me as if she hasn't heard my question. "Could you repeat the question?" she sniffs.

"Has your daughter been seeing a therapist?"

"No, she hasn't."

I love her snippiness and I pray she gives me a lot more of it.

"If she was so devastated by what happened, why hasn't she been in therapy?"

"Are you trying to say this didn't affect my baby?"

"I'm sorry, Mrs. Carlyle, I'm the one asking the questions. I'm just trying to understand why you haven't placed your daughter in therapy."

"We haven't found the right therapist."

"How many therapists have you interviewed?"

She glares over at Sullivan as if she's being derelict for not objecting. "Isn't that confidential information?"

"Again, Mrs. Carlyle, I'm the one asking the questions. I don't want to know any specifics about her therapy—which *would* be confidential. I just want to know how many therapists you've spoken to in an effort to get help for your daughter."

Mrs. Carlyle puckers her lips and shifts in her seat. She steals another look at Sullivan, who's looking quite alarmed herself. Her opening witness was supposed to pull at the jury's heartstrings.

"If you must know, my husband doesn't believe in therapy. He's a very private person. We're dealing with this through our faith."

I peek over my shoulder at Mr. Carlyle, knowing the jurors will follow my gaze. Percy Carlyle looks even more uncomfortable than his wife. He tugs at his tie for the third time.

"Okay, what church do you attend?"

"Objection, Your Honor," Sullivan says. "This is really going far afield."

"No, Your Honor, it isn't. Mrs. Carlyle just testified that they're dealing with the situation through their faith. I'm just trying to confirm that."

"I'll allow it," Lipscomb says, "but not for too much longer."

"Holman United Methodist Church," she says proudly.

Holman is one of the most prominent black churches in L.A. Something tells me Simone just snatched that name out of the air.

"And where is that church located?"

"In Los Angeles."

"On what street?"

"I don't understand why that's relevant," Simone snarls.

*It's relevant because you don't even know where the church is, which proves you're a big fat liar.*

"Do you know what street the church is on, Mrs. Carlyle?"

She shoots daggers at me. "It's very stressful sitting up here in this witness box. I'm sorry, but I can't remember right now."

"Does Adams Boulevard ring a bell?"

She smiles. "Oh, yes, it's on Adams."

"And who's the head minister there?"

If looks could kill, I'd be dead. She doesn't know that either.

"Isn't Reverend Sauls the minister there?" I say, helping her out again.

"Yes, that's it. Reverend Sauls."

"And when is the last time your family went to church?"

Her eyes narrow into slits. "Just because we don't go to church every Sunday doesn't mean we don't have faith."

*C'mon, girlfriend, keep it coming!*

"That wasn't my question, Mrs. Carlyle. I asked when your family last visited Holman United Methodist Church."

"I don't remember."

"Have you been since the day you learned about the picture of your daughter?"

"No, we haven't and I don't appreciate what you're trying to imply. My daughter is suffering and we're doing everything we can to help her."

I stand there long enough to check out the frowns in the jury box. A couple of women even shake their heads. I've done my job.

"I have no further questions for this witness."

As soon as I'm seated, Jenny leans across Graylin. "Great cross," she says. "How'd you know they didn't go to church?"

"Because that woman is too evil to step foot into a church."

# CHAPTER 46

## *Angela*

After the break, Sullivan calls Officer Fenton to the witness stand. His testimony on direct and cross is much the same as it was during the preliminary hearing. Sullivan doesn't call Officer Chin, at all. Probably because she doesn't want the jury to see him for the liar that he is.

To support the witness intimidation charge, Sullivan produces Little Slice's cousin, who claims he made the call to Kennedy on Graylin's behalf. On cross, I establish that he never spoke to Graylin and that the prosecution didn't pursue any charges against him in exchange for his testimony.

I'm surprised when Kennedy and her father don't return to the courtroom after the break, but minutes later, I understand why. Sullivan calls a computer specialist from the D.A.'s Office to testify that the naked picture of Kennedy was retrieved from Graylin's phone. When the picture appears on the huge courtroom screen, her breasts and groin area are blacked out.

I hate the reaction of the jurors. More than a few shake their heads. Graylin stares down at his hands, never looking at the picture. Mrs. Carlyle, of course, is there to put on a weeping show.

Sullivan's next witness is LaShay Baker, who's accompanied by her grandmother. Mama Baker strolls into court wearing her Sunday best. She's decked out in a red, hip-clinging knit skirt suit with a hat that resembles a sombrero.

When the bailiff calls LaShay to the stand, the whole courtroom can hear Mama Baker's raspy voice even though she's trying to whisper. "Don't be afraid, baby. Just tell the truth. The truth shall set you free."

LaShay states her name for the record and explains that she's Kennedy's best friend. Sullivan starts with an area that catches us totally by surprise.

"Did you ever see the defendant bullying Kennedy?"

"Um, yes."

"How did he bully Kennedy?"

"He and Crayvon Little, that's another boy in our class, they would make jokes about her."

Graylin *and* Crayvon. This is news to us.

Graylin is incensed. "She's lying on me, Ms. Angela!" he whispers.

I place my hand on Graylin's forearm. He heeds my signal and calms down, but I know it won't be for long.

"What kind of jokes?"

"They would say she's skinny and that her weave looks like horse hair and that she's stuck-up."

"And how did Kennedy react when they did that?"

"She would cry because her feelings would be hurt."

Right on cue, I can hear Simone Carlyle sniffling.

"Do you know if Graylin ever showed the picture of Kennedy to anyone?"

"Yes."

Jenny and I lean forward at the same time.

"Who did he show it to?"

"I was walking behind Graylin as we were leaving first-period class. I heard him tell Crayvon he had a picture he wanted to show him."

"And then what happened?"

"Crayvon said he couldn't look at it right then because he had to go to the administration office."

"And was there another time when Graylin tried to get Crayvon to look at the picture?"

"Yes. During first period when we were taking our algebra test. Graylin made a spitball and threw it at Crayvon. When he turned around, Graylin held up his phone and pointed at it. But Crayvon was trying to finish his test and ignored him."

I look over at Graylin. Whenever someone says something that isn't true, Graylin reacts with pure outrage. Right now, he's quiet, which tells me that LaShay is speaking the truth.

"Thank you, LaShay," Sullivan says. "I have no further questions."

I'm not quite sure how I want to play this. It's almost four o'clock and the jury looks as exhausted as I am. I need to make my cross quick.

"LaShay, how long have you known Graylin?"

"Since elementary school."

"Do you think Graylin's a nice boy?"

"Yes, ma'am, he's pretty nice. And he's smart too."

"When you said Graylin and Crayvon made jokes about Kennedy, wasn't it only Crayvon making those jokes?"

"Yes, ma'am. Graylin was just there with him."

"Then why did you say Graylin and Crayvon made jokes about Kennedy?"

She looks over at Sullivan. "Um, Ms. Prosecutor asked me if Graylin was there when Crayvon made the jokes and I said yes. So she said that means they were doing it together."

Sullivan cringes like she wants to crawl under the table. The judge is glaring at her, and so is the entire jury.

"So, you never heard Graylin make any jokes about Kennedy, correct?"

"Yes, that's correct."

"You testified that Graylin told Crayvon he had a picture to show him. But isn't it true that Graylin only said he had something to show Crayvon, never mentioning a picture?"

She stops to think. "Yeah, maybe."

It's too dangerous to question her about Graylin holding up his phone in class. So I move on.

"Do you think Crayvon has a crush on Kennedy?"

"Yes, he—"

"Objection, calls for speculation."

"Sustained."

I quickly rephrase the question. "Did Crayvon ever do anything that made you think he liked Kennedy?"

"Yes, ma'am. He was always liking her pictures on Instagram. He tried to get her to instant message him, but she wouldn't."

I know I'm going to get an objection to my next question, but I ask it anyway. "Do you think Crayvon tried to embarrass Kennedy because she rejected him?"

"Objection, Your Honor." This time Sullivan is more than pissed. "Calls for speculation."

"Sustained."

"Did you ever see Graylin do anything to hurt Kennedy's feelings?"

"Um, no ma'am. Graylin's nice. Everybody likes him."

That's the best I'm going to get. I slowly walk back to the defense table.

"I have no further questions of this witness, Your Honor."

# CHAPTER 47

## *Angela*

I've been expecting a surprise or two from Sullivan, but not this one.

As soon as we enter the courtroom for day two of the trial, Sullivan hands me a revised witness list.

"I just added two new witnesses," she says with a surprisingly straight face. "The late notice shouldn't be a problem since they're on your witness list."

"Who are they?" Jenny says, reading the document over my shoulder as Sullivan walks away.

"Taisha and Crayvon."

"Why would Sullivan want to call either of them?" Jenny asks. "Especially Taisha. It's going to hurt her case when she testifies that Crayvon went into Kennedy's backyard by himself."

I have a bad feeling. Sullivan's a very skilled attorney. She wouldn't knowingly offer testimony that could raise reasonable doubt.

Ten minutes later, Taisha Davis saunters down the center aisle of the courtroom like a mutant ninja midget. She's dressed in green from head to toe. Green pants, green blouse, green earrings, even green eye shadow and fingernail polish. From the smile on her face, it's clear that she loves being the center of attention.

Taisha is sworn in and Sullivan approaches her like they're old friends.

"Good morning. May I call you Taisha?"

"Yes, you may." Taisha daintily clasps her hands in her lap.

"Do you know the defendant Graylin Alexander?"

"Yes, he's best friends with a boy who lives on my street named Crayvon Little."

"Do you know Kennedy Carlyle?"

"Yeah, she lives on my street too."

"Have you ever been in her house?"

"Yep, lots of times."

Sullivan puts a picture up on the courtroom screen.

"Is this Kennedy's house?"

"Yes."

"Where is Kennedy's bedroom?"

"In the back on the first floor, just like at my house."

Sullivan draws Taisha's attention to another picture. "And is this a picture of Kennedy's backyard?"

"Yes."

"Can you point to Kennedy's bedroom?"

"It's the window on the right."

"During the week of May tenth, did you see Graylin sneaking into Kennedy's backyard?"

"I sure did."

A couple of jurors gasp. Taisha smiles and pauses like she's taking cues from a Hollywood director.

I place a hand on Graylin's forearm. "Remember, the jury is watching you. Don't show your emotions. Stay calm."

"Can you tell us what you saw?"

"I was looking out of our living room window and I saw Graylin and his friend Crayvon sneaking into Kennedy's backyard. Her house is right across the street from mine."

"How long were they in the backyard?"

"About five minutes, I guess."

"After they came out, did one of them go back there alone?"

"Yep, Crayvon went home. Then Graylin went back there a few minutes later by himself."

"Ms. Angela!" Graylin whispers way too loudly. "She's lying on me!"

Jenny admonishes him before I can. "We know, Graylin. You have to be quiet so we can hear what she's saying."

"And did you learn that Graylin was arrested for having a naked picture of Kennedy Carlyle a couple of days later?" Sullivan asks.

"Yes."

"I have no further questions."

I'm stunned by Sullivan's lightning-fast examination. She has to know she's only getting half of the story.

Graylin is near tears. "I never went back there by myself, Ms. Angela. I swear! Why is Taisha lying on me?"

"I don't know," I say, getting to my feet. "But I'm about to find out."

As I'm walking toward the jury box to face Taisha, Jenny blasts out of her seat like a missile.

"Your Honor, please forgive me for the interruption. I need to speak to my co-counsel. Right now."

Judge Lipscomb grimaces. "Make it quick."

Jenny's interruption has wrecked my rhythm. Whatever she has to say better be important. As I turn around, I pray the jury doesn't see the angst on my face.

I take the few short steps back to the defense table.

Before I can ask her what's up, Jenny grips my forearm so hard I think it might snap in two. "We missed it!" she whispers into my ear.

"Missed what? And why couldn't you wait until I—"

"Crayvon didn't do it!" Jenny declares. "It's Taisha. Taisha took that picture and sent it to Graylin!"

# CHAPTER **48**

## *Angela*

It takes me a few seconds to process this. Taisha lives across the street from Kennedy. Taisha was the one Kennedy kicked to the curb. Taisha lies like a rug. Taisha had means, motive, and opportunity.

I turn back around to face the witness box, my heart racing. "May I also call you Taisha?"

"Yes, you may."

"Did you speak with my investigator, a woman named, Mei?"

"Yep. A cute Asian girl, right?"

"Yes."

"Yep, I spoke to her. I saw her sneaking into Kennedy's back-yard too. The same day she interviewed me."

This little girl is dangerous. I have to keep this moving.

"Didn't you tell my investigator that it was Crayvon who returned and went back there by himself, not Graylin?"

"Nope."

"And didn't—" I'm on to another question before I realize that Taisha didn't give me the answer I was expecting.

"What did you say?"

"You have your facts wrong. I never saw Crayvon go into Kennedy's backyard by himself. Just Graylin."

"You do understand that you're under oath, correct?"

"Yes."

Since I'm facing a lying witness, I have to tread lightly.

"You have no idea whether Kennedy was home on the day you *claim* you saw Graylin and Crayvon going into her backyard, correct?"

"Nope. I'm pretty sure she was home."

*You little tart.*

"Didn't you tell my investigator that you didn't know whether she was home or not?"

"Nope. I told her Kennedy was at home."

"Taisha, you're in foster care, correct?"

"Yes."

"Who is your foster mother?"

"Mrs. Betty Taylor."

Mrs. Taylor isn't in the courtroom. Maybe Taisha wouldn't be lying if she was here.

"Was your foster mother home the day you spoke with our investigator?"

"Yes."

"And didn't your foster mother tell the investigator that you have a habit of lying?"

"I don't know what she told her. I wasn't listening to their conversation. They told me to go back inside."

"Well, do you have a habit of lying?"

For the first time, Taisha pauses to think about her answer. "I wouldn't call it lying. Sometimes I remember things or forget things."

"Are you forgetting something about the day you claim you saw Graylin and Crayvon going into Kennedy's backyard?"

"Nope. I saw Graylin go back there by himself. That's what I saw with my own two eyes."

"You don't know what Graylin and Crayvon were doing in Kennedy's backyard, correct?"

"Not really. But when Graylin went back there by himself, I did see a phone in his hand."

I cross my arms and pause. I can't let the jury see how irritated I am with this little girl.

"You have no evidence that Graylin took any pictures in Kennedy's backyard, correct?"

"He must've. Kennedy's picture ended up on his phone."

"Objection," I say. "Move to strike the witness' statement as speculation."

"Sustained."

"You didn't actually see Graylin take a picture. You're just guessing, correct?"

She shrugs.

"I didn't hear you."

"No, I didn't see him do it. But the police must've arrested him for a reason."

"Again, Your Honor, move to strike."

"Sustained," Judge Lipscomb says. "Young lady, we don't want you to guess."

Taisha smiles up at him. "Okay, judge."

It's time for me to turn on her. "You took that picture of Kennedy, didn't you?"

Taisha doesn't even blink. "Nope."

"You were upset with Kennedy for not being your friend anymore, weren't you?"

"I don't care about her. I have lots of friends."

"Name them?"

"What?"

"Name your friends."

Taisha flubs.

Sullivan jumps to her defense. "Your Honor, counsel's badgering the witness."

"Sustained."

"You wanted to hurt Kennedy, didn't you?"

"You're not going to pin this on me," Taisha says calmly. "I didn't do it. Graylin did."

I stare at her a few seconds, then turn away. "I have no further questions."

Sullivan almost crashes into the witness box in her rush to rehabilitate her star witness.

"Just a few questions, Taisha. Do you have a computer at home?"

"No."

"Do you have a cell phone?"

"No."

"Do you have a Snapchat account?"

"Nope."

"No more questions, Your Honor."

As Taisha saunters past our table, she looks as if she's about to stick out her tongue at me. Instead, she flashes me a cheeky smile.

Judge Lipscomb bangs his gavel. "Let's take a ten-minute break. And I mean ten minutes, not a second longer."

"She's lying!" Graylin bursts into a full-blown crying fit as soon as the jury is ushered out of the courtroom. "I never went back there by myself. Why did she lie on me like that, Ms. Angela?"

"I don't know." I point him toward the back of the courtroom. "Why don't you go talk to your dad and your granny?"

After Graylin walks away, I tell Jenny we need to call Taisha's foster mother to testify about her proclivity for lying. "How do you think the jury reacted to me going after her?"

"I'm sure they don't think she's credible," Jenny says. "I can't believe we didn't focus on her earlier."

I'm not entirely onboard with Jenny's theory about Taisha. My bet is still on Crayvon and I hope we haven't hurt ourselves by zeroing in on her.

"Something's not right," I say.

Jenny furrows her perfectly arched eyebrows. "What are you talking about?"

"I have a bad feeling that Sullivan has an even bigger surprise for us when Crayvon takes the witness stand."

# CHAPTER 49

## *Angela*

The trial is taking its toll on Graylin. All morning, he's been asking us the same question over and over again.

"Ms. Angela, if Crayvon lies on me too, you have to let me testify so I can tell the jury I didn't do it. You're going to let me testify, right?"

"We'll see," I say yet again.

We've explained to Graylin that it's not usually a good idea for defendants to testify. But since Taisha's testimony, getting the truth out is all he's been able to focus on. Too bad this process has very little to do with the truth.

Once the jurors are seated, Judge Lipscomb instructs Sullivan to call her next witness.

The bailiff retrieves Crayvon Little from the hallway. Unlike Taisha, he walks unsteadily down the aisle toward the witness stand. He's wearing a brown suit and shoes that look as if they've been polished with Vaseline. While LaShay and Taisha were almost swallowed up by the witness box, Crayvon sits tall.

After establishing his age, where he lives and attends school, Sullivan moves on to questions that will score her some points.

"Crayvon, how long have you known Graylin Alexander?"

Crayvon clears his throat. "A long time. Since third grade."

"Is he one of your closest friends?"

"Yes."

"Not anymore," Graylin mutters under his breath.

"To your knowledge, did Graylin have a crush on Kennedy Carlyle?"

Crayvon sits up straighter. "Yes."

Graylin flinches. "He's lying, Ms. Angela! He likes her, not me!"

I squeeze Graylin's arm. He says something indecipherable and quiets down.

"How did you know Graylin had a crush on Kennedy?"

"Because he told me he liked her."

"Did you like Kennedy?"

"No. I have a girlfriend. Her name is Danielle. She goes to my church."

"Did Graylin ever visit your home?"

"Yep, all the time."

"Do you live on the same street as Kennedy Carlyle?"

"Yes."

"During the week of May tenth, did you and the defendant, Graylin Alexander, sneak into Kennedy's backyard?"

"Yes."

"Why did you do that?"

"We were just looking around. We ran back out after a few minutes."

"Was Kennedy at home?"

"I don't know."

"Did you look into her bedroom window?"

"No."

"How long were you and Graylin in her backyard?"

"Not long. Only a few minutes."

"Did you have your cell phone with you?"

"No."

"Did Graylin have his cell phone with him?"

"Yes."

"After you left the backyard, what did you do?"

"We went back to my house and watched TV, but then Graylin had to leave so he could get home before it got dark."

"Did Graylin have to pass by Kennedy's house on his way home?"

"Yes."

"Did Graylin ever tell you he had a naked picture of Kennedy on his phone?"

"Kinda."

"What do you mean?"

"He tried to show it to me, but I had to take something to the administration office for my teacher, so I couldn't see it."

"When was this?"

"The same day he got arrested. Right before our second-period class started. And in first period, when we were taking our algebra test, he threw a spitball at me to get my attention. When I looked back at him, he was holding up his phone and pointing at it. He was trying to tell me something, but I didn't understand at the time. But now I know he was—"

Jenny is on her feet. "Objection, calls for speculation. The witness just testified that he didn't understand what Graylin was trying to tell him."

We decided last night that Jenny would handle the cross of Crayvon since she has more experience with child witnesses.

"Sustained," Judge Lipscomb says.

Sullivan doesn't mind the objection. The jury will infer that Graylin was trying to show him the picture of Kennedy.

"What did you do when Graylin tried to get your attention?"

"I didn't want to talk because I was trying to concentrate on my test. So I ignored him."

"Did you take the picture of Kennedy and send it to Graylin?"

"No. I didn't have nothing to do with any of this."

Sullivan nods. "I have no further questions of this witness."

Jenny smiles as she approaches Crayvon.

"How many days was it between the time the two of you went into Kennedy's backyard and Graylin's arrest?"

"Three days."

"So if someone else testified that it was two days, would they be wrong?"

"Yep. I know it was three days because I watched *NCIS* later that night and it comes on on Tuesday nights."

"Do you talk to Graylin on the phone?"

"No, we usually text."

"Did Graylin text you after he left your house that day?"

"Probably."

"Did he mention taking a picture of Kennedy?"

"Nope."

"When was the next time you saw Graylin?"

"The next day, Wednesday, in first period."

"Did he mention taking a picture of Kennedy?"

"No."

"And when you saw him in the cafeteria at lunchtime, did he tell you that he had a picture of Kennedy?"

"No."

"Did he tell you anytime that day that he had a picture of Kennedy?"

"No."

"Did he tell you anytime on Thursday that he had a picture of Kennedy?"

"No."

"What about before your algebra test on Friday? Did Graylin tell you then that he had a picture of Kennedy?"

"No."

"So if Graylin had taken a picture of Kennedy after school on Tuesday, do you think he would've waited all the way until Friday to show it to you?"

This time Sullivan interrupts. "Objection, calls for speculation."

"Sustained."

"Probably not," Crayvon says, not understanding the objection.

"Young man," the judge says, "if I say an objection is sustained, that means you shouldn't answer the question."

"Okay, sorry."

"Did you ever tease Kennedy about being skinny?"

He scratches his jaw. "Sometimes, but I was only playing around."

"Did you ever tease her about wearing a weave?"

"Yeah, but I didn't mean any harm."

"Did you ever call her stuck-up?"

"I guess so."

"Did you ever tell LaShay that you wanted Kennedy to be your girlfriend?"

"No. I already have a girlfriend."

"It made you mad that Kennedy rejected you, didn't it?"

Crayvon's nose twitches and his lips protrude. "No! I didn't like her. Nobody likes her. She thinks she's better than everybody else because her parents have a lot of money."

Jenny walks over to the defense table and lifts a few pages of her legal pad. She's not looking at anything in particular. She's letting Crayvon's heated words hang in the air.

"Did a girl at your church named Nedra Johnson accuse you of putting your hand underneath her dress?"

This question catches both Crayvon and Sullivan by surprise.

Crayvon's head whips back. "That was—I was—she lied on me."

"So did you put your hand underneath her dress?"

He briefly averts his eyes, making him look like the liar that he is. "No."

Sullivan finally snaps out of her fog. "Objection, Your Honor. Asking this witness about an unfounded allegation is far more prejudicial than probative. I move to strike the witness' answer and request an instruction to the jury."

"Sustained." Judge Lipscomb glances over at the jurors. "The jury should disregard both the question and the witness' response."

I smile. That instruction is absolutely worthless. The genie is already out of the bottle.

"Did you ever go into Kennedy's backyard and take a picture through her bedroom window?"

"No, I did not."

"Do you have a Snapchat account?"

"I used to. But my mama made me get off Snapchat after what happened to Graylin."

"Did you ever send a naked picture of Kennedy to Graylin on Snapchat?"

"No!"

"You didn't want to see the picture Graylin was trying to show you because you were the one who sent it to him, isn't that correct?"

"No, it's not!"

"You were the one who left that anonymous note in the administration office, weren't you?"

His eyes expand and he's on the verge of tears. "No! I told you I had nothing to do with it!"

Jenny backs off and asks him about his grades. At first I'm stunned, then I get it. If Crayvon starts crying, the jury is likely to feel sorry for him. She asks a few more benign questions, then moves on to motive.

"When is the last time you saw your father?"

He shrugs. "I don't know."

"Are you close to your father?"

"Not really."

"Is Graylin close to his father?"

"Yeah."

"Didn't Graylin's father"—Jenny turns to smile at Gus, who we positioned one row behind the defense table today—"often take you along when he took Graylin out?"

Crayvon shrugs. "Yeah, I guess so."

"Where did you go with Gus and Graylin?"

"The movies."

"And where else?"

"The park and fishing and stuff like that."

"Didn't Graylin's father buy him a leather jacket and get you one too?"

"Yeah."

"You're jealous of Graylin because he's close to his father, aren't you?"

Crayvon's anger resurfaces like a high tide. "I'm not jealous of him! At least my father's not an ex-con!"

Jenny stifles a smile. Crayvon couldn't sound more envious if we'd written him a script. She walks back to her notes, waits a long beat, then turns to the judge.

"Your Honor, I have no more questions for this witness."

# CHAPTER 50

## *Angela*

Jenny and I are standing at the defense table about to head out for lunch when Sullivan walks over.

"We're dropping the criminal threat and distribution charges," she says, in the same tone she might use to tell us what she had for lunch.

This is good news, but not quite good enough. "The witness intimidation and invasion of privacy charges should go too," I say. "There's no evidence to support them either."

Sullivan shrugs. "Those stay."

I feel like an angry bull taunted by a flash of red. She's produced no evidence showing Graylin took the picture of Kennedy. Nor has any witness credibly tied Graylin to the threatening call Kennedy received. The only reason she's not dropping that charge is because without it, Judge Lipscomb would no longer have jurisdiction over this case and we'd be kicked back to juvenile court.

I take a step into Sullivan's personal space. "How do you sleep at night? You can't just—"

Jenny slips between us. "Thanks for the heads-up," she tells Sullivan as she drags me out of the courtroom and into the hallway.

My eyes well with tears. It's not like me to behave that way toward an opposing counsel.

"Please chill," Jenny says, throwing an arm around my shoulder. "You've been kicking butt. No matter how many games the prosecution plays, we're still winning."

I only wish I had Jenny's confidence.

We all gather at a sandwich shop, where I tell Gus and Graylin about two of the charges being dropped. Graylin is thrilled and more convinced than ever that he's going to win.

When it's time to return to court, Jenny tries to cheer me up. "Let it go. Sullivan hasn't met her burden and she knows it. We scored some major points with Crayvon today."

"What major points?"

"What fourteen-year-old boy who takes a naked picture of his classmate on Tuesday is going to wait until Friday to show it to his best friend. If that doesn't raise reasonable doubt, I don't know what will."

By the time the jury is called back in, it's well after one o'clock. The judge directs me to call my first witness. We only have three. Taisha's foster mother, Graylin's minister, and one of his teachers.

Betty Taylor does an excellent job of explaining that Taisha's excessive lying is a cry for attention. Next, Graylin's science teacher calls him one of the best students she's had in her twenty-plus years of teaching. For almost fifteen minutes, Reverend Ball praises Graylin as a real leader and a blessing to his church.

I'm about to move on to Graylin's work helping the homeless when Mama Baker storms into the courtroom, dragging her granddaughter LaShay by the forearm.

"The devil is a lie! The devil is a lie!" she yells. "Mama Baker don't raise no heathens!"

Judge Lipscomb bangs his gavel. "What the hell? Order in the court! Order in the court!"

"Judge," Mama Baker says, waving her free hand, "we need to have a little talk because Mama Baker don't raise no heathens. My granddaughter needs to get back up on that witness stand. And the sooner the better!"

Mama Baker is about to step into the well of the courtroom when the slow-moving bailiff jogs over and blocks her path.

"I need to talk to the judge," she says. "Because the devil is a lie!"

Judge Lipscomb looks as flustered as the bailiff. "Mrs. Baker, you can't interrupt a court proceeding like this. Please leave my courtroom."

"I prayed on this all night, judge, and this is what the Lord told me to do."

"Get the jury out of here!" Judge Lipscomb says to the bailiff. "Ma'am, please don't say another word."

The jurors snicker as they file through the door behind the jury box. Once they're gone, the judge erupts.

"This is highly inappropriate. I just may find you in contempt of court."

"That's good and well, but you should know that Jesus is the only judge I fear. My granddaughter didn't tell the truth up there on that witness stand. And I can't let that be. She needs to redo her testimony because Mama Baker don't raise no heathens."

LaShay cowers behind her grandmother, her face wet with tears.

The judge is at a loss for words. He's obviously never had to face anyone like Mama Baker before.

"I'd like to see counsel and Mrs. Baker in my chambers. Now!"

# Chapter 51

## Angela

When we finish listening to what Mama Baker has to say, everybody in Judge Lipscomb's chambers is flabbergasted.

The judge orders Mama Baker back to the courtroom. He looks at Sullivan, then at Jenny and me. "How would you like to proceed?"

"I'd like to request a mistrial," Sullivan says in a voice stripped of emotion.

"We don't want a mistrial," I say. "We want a dismissal."

Sullivan hesitates. "What we just heard doesn't impact the possession charge."

"Then let's proceed," I say, more fired up than ever. "I'd like to recall LaShay to the witness stand right now. I can finish up the reverend later."

The judge shakes his head. "In my twenty-three years on the bench this is the craziest thing I've ever seen."

He gives us ten minutes to talk to Gus and Graylin, who also don't want a mistrial.

"What did LaShay's granny say, Ms. Angela? Did she tell the judge Crayvon and Taisha lied on me?"

"Hold on. You'll find out everything in a second."

I start scribbling down notes for my cross-examination of LaShay. I don't have time to write down complete questions, so I jot down key words as reminders of the areas I want to cover. I pass my legal pad to Jenny. She peruses it then scribbles down another topic for me to address.

Judge Lipscomb calls the jury back in and LaShay walks to the jury box. The judge reminds her that she's still under oath. The little girl's eyes are puffy and red.

"LaShay, when you testified in this courtroom yesterday, did you tell the truth?" I begin.

Her head is bowed so low that her chin grazes her chest. "No, ma'am."

"Are you ready to tell the truth now?"

"Yes, ma'am."

"Do you know who took the naked picture of your friend Kennedy Carlyle?"

LaShay nods.

"I'm sorry, LaShay. You'll need to speak up so the jury and the court reporter can hear you."

"Um, yes, I know."

"Please tell the jury who took it."

"I did."

The collective gasp is so loud it sounds like the courtroom is equipped with surround sound. I wait for the commotion to die down before continuing.

"And why did you take a naked picture of Kennedy?"

"Because she asked me to."

Mrs. Carlyle jumps to her feet. "That's a lie! You framed that boy, and now you're trying to frame my baby!"

The bailiff trots over to Simone just as Mama Baker revs up.

"The devil is a lie!" she yells from the back row. "The truth shall set you free. Go ahead, baby. Bare your soul. Jesus loves you."

The judge bangs his gavel and points it first at Mrs. Carlyle, then at Mama Baker. "If I hear another peep from either one of you, you're both out of here!"

The bailiff is in the middle of the aisle, an arm's reach away from both of them.

I move closer to the witness box, hoping to make LaShay feel more at ease.

"So why did Kennedy ask you to take a naked picture of her?"

"She wanted to get back at Graylin for not liking her. She knew he would get in trouble if he had a naked picture of her."

"Do you know who left the note for the principal?"

"Um, yes. Kennedy typed it up, but I left it on the counter when nobody was looking."

"When did you do that?"

"Right before second period started."

"Do you know who sent Graylin the picture on Snapchat?"

"Yeah. Kennedy did that part. She made up a fake Snapchat account. There's a website you can go to and get a fake email address that nobody can trace."

"Did she send the picture to anybody else besides Graylin?"

"Yeah, lots of people, but Graylin got it first. She told me she wanted it to go viral so she would get famous like Kim Kardashian. I don't think she thought it would really go viral because when it did, she got scared. We also didn't know Graylin would get in trouble with the police. We thought he would only get detention or something like that."

I think I have everything I need. I glance back at Jenny for confirmation. She nods.

"I have no further questions, Your Honor."

For the first time, Sullivan looks deflated. She places both hands flat on the table and pushes herself to her feet.

"LaShay, are you certain you're telling the truth?"

"Yes, ma'am."

"Is this the truth or is this what your grandmother told you to say?"

Mama Baker is on her feet. "The devil is a lie! The truth—"

The judge bangs his gavel. "That's it. Bailiff, show Mrs. Baker out of my courtroom."

Mama Baker keeps talking as she waddles down the aisle. "That's okay, baby. You just tell 'em the truth. The truth shall set you free."

Sullivan swallows and resumes. "You claim Kennedy wanted to get Graylin in trouble, correct?"

"Yes."

"How did she know he would take a screenshot of the picture?"

LaShay looks at Sullivan as if the question doesn't make sense. "Because everybody does."

Sullivan opens her mouth to speak, then apparently thinks better of it. "I have no further questions of this witness, Your Honor."

"I think that's enough for today," the judge says. "I'm dismissing the jury and I'd like to see counsel in my chambers."

"Did we win, Ms. Angela?" Graylin says, excited. "Is that why you have to go talk to the judge?"

I'm praying that's the case, but I don't want to get his hopes up. "I don't know, Graylin. We'll have to see."

I feel a hand on my shoulder and turn around to an embrace from Gus. "Dre told me you would do it!"

I eye Dre over my shoulder at the back of the courtroom. He's smiling with such pride that it warms me up inside. Gus hugs Jenny too.

"Let's not count our chickens before they're hatched," I say. "I wish I could take all the credit, but this was nothing short of divine intervention."

When we enter the judge's chambers, he's stripping off his robe.

"Ms. Sullivan," Judge Lipscomb says, as he sits down behind his desk, "you have some decisions to make regarding the charges against this defendant."

Sullivan looks down at the floor.

"Do you want to proceed with this prosecution," he asks, "or dismiss the case?"

"Let me talk to my boss." She sounds as if all the life has been sucked out of her. "I'll have a decision in the morning."

As soon as we reenter the courtroom, Gus and Graylin run up to us.

"What happened in there?" Gus asks.

"I have a strong feeling the charges are going to be dismissed," I say. "The prosecutor has to check with her boss. We'll know for sure in the morning.

"I told you guys! Little Slice was right! If I had stayed in juvenile court, that judge would've locked me up and made me a sex offender! Now I'm going free!"

Jenny smiles. "I don't know about y'all, but I think we should do some early celebrating."

# CHAPTER 52

## *Angela*

We give Graylin the honor of picking the restaurant and he chooses El Torito in Marina Del Rey. An hour later, we're all seated at a long table, munching on chips and salsa, drinking margaritas and gazing at the sailboats docked along the Marina.

I can't explain how great it feels to see Graylin so happy.

"*The devil is a lie! The devil is a lie!*" he exclaims every few minutes. "*Mama Baker don't raise no heathens!* LaShay's grandmama was so funny."

"You need to be thanking God that she's an honest woman," I tell him. "Not everybody would've done what she did."

"I can't believe this nightmare is finally over," Gus says. "If I ever catch a case again, I'm calling the two of you."

A waitress sets a bowl of guacamole and two platters of chicken quesadillas in the middle of the table.

Graylin lifts his strawberry lemonade high in the air. "A toast to the two best attorneys in the whole wide world!"

We all raise our glasses in cheer.

"So what's going to happen to Kennedy and LaShay?" Dre asks. "They're the ones who should face child pornography charges."

"I don't know," I say. "I suspect the D.A.'s Office just wants this case to go away."

"Hell, naw," Gus bellows. "That D.A. better file charges against both of 'em."

"It's likely Kennedy and LaShay will be charged," Jenny says. "Especially if you push for it."

"I plan to," Gus says. "And I also plan to sue both of those girls and their parents, just like that witch Simone said she was going to do me. Me and my son want some emotional distress money for everything they put us through."

My phone rings and *No Caller ID* shows up on the display. My pulse speeds up. Calls from the prosecutor's office usually show up that way.

"Hey, everybody, this might be the prosecutor." I wave my hand in the air so they all quiet down.

I place the phone to my ear, but I'm having a hard time hearing over the restaurant noise.

"Hold on a minute," I say into the phone. "Let me put my earphones in so I can hear you better."

I listen for about a minute, then hang up. Everyone is smiling in anticipation of what I have to say. But Dre knows me and immediately senses that something is wrong.

He squeezes my shoulder. "Babe, what did she say?"

"They're dropping the charges." I pause, not wanting to relay the rest of the conversation. "All of them except for the possession of child pornography charge."

"Are you friggin' kidding me?" Gus slams his fist on the table so hard that water splashes out of his glass.

"Sullivan's offering Graylin a deferred entry of judgment deal."

"What's that?" Dre asks.

"Graylin has to plead guilty to the possession charge," I explain. "If he goes to school and stays out of trouble for a year, the charge will be dismissed. But if he gets in any kind of trouble during that time, the deal is revoked and he'll be placed on probation." I pause. "Until he's twenty-one."

"Twenty-one!" Gus screeches. "That's nuts!"

"Hold on," Jenny says. "That's the worst-case scenario. It's rare for probation to actually last that long."

"And if he does something that violates his probation," Dre presses, "then what happens?"

Jenny inhales long and hard. "He'll have to provide a sample of his DNA to police so that if he commits a crime in the future, it's in the system. The police will have the right to search his person and his home at any time without a warrant and without probable cause. He'll also have a felony on his record, have to serve time—probably in a juvenile camp—and have to register as a sex offender."

"We have to consider the offer," I say. "If Graylin's convicted, he could—"

"No!" Graylin yells. Tears dampen his cheeks. "I'm not pleading guilty to nothing because I'm not a child pornographer!"

I turn to Jenny and know instantly that we are on the same page. There's no disputing that Graylin was in possession of child pornography. The law doesn't care how he got it. The only way we can win on the remaining charge is via jury nullification, which always was and still is a gamble.

"Graylin," Jenny says gently, "this is a good thing."

"No it isn't!" he shouts, his tears streaming now. "That jury isn't going to convict me. Not after you showed them how everybody lied on me. You said I'm the client, so it's my decision. I'm taking my chances with the jury."

# CHAPTER 53

## *Angela*

When Judge Lipscomb calls the attorneys into his chambers the next morning, it feels like we're marching in a funeral procession.

"So where do we stand?" he asks. He's sitting forward in his chair, his elbows propped on his desk.

Sullivan shuffles from one foot to the other. "We're dropping the invasion of privacy and witness intimidation charges," she says. "But we're proceeding with the possession of child pornography charge."

The judge squints up at her. "You're kidding me, right?"

Sullivan blows out a breath. "Your Honor, there's no disputing that the defendant saved the picture to his phone."

"And there's also no disputing that Penal Code 311 was intended to go after pedophiles and this kid is no pedophile. If you're dropping the witness intimidation charge, that means I no longer have jurisdiction. Therefore, I can send this case back to juvenile court where it belongs."

"We did offer the defendant a deferred entry of judgment deal," Sullivan says. "But he turned it down."

Now the judge is giving me the same scolding look he'd just given Sullivan.

"Ms. Evans, please tell me you didn't advise your client not to take the deal."

"Your Honor, we've tried everything, but Graylin won't agree to it. His father couldn't convince him either."

The judge grunts. "Get him in here. His father too."

I walk back into the courtroom to retrieve them.

"Why does the judge want to speak to me, Ms. Angela?"

"Because he's not happy that you turned down the prosecutor's offer."

"I sure hope the judge can talk some sense into this stubborn fool," Gus mutters.

Graylin takes a seat in front of the judge's desk. His father stands behind him, gripping the back of his chair.

"Good morning, young man." Judge Lipscomb rounds his desk and sits on the edge, facing Graylin. "Explain to me what Ms. Sullivan offered you. I want to make sure you understand what you're turning down."

"If I plead guilty and stay out of trouble for a year, then the possessing child pornography charge will be dismissed. But if I do something wrong, I'll be locked up and be a sex offender and have to give the police my DNA."

"I'm sure a good kid like you can stay out of trouble for a year. Don't you think the prosecutor is offering you a good deal?"

Graylin exhales. "No, sir."

"Why not?"

"Because I'm not a child pornographer and I shouldn't have to plead guilty to something I didn't do."

Judge Lipscomb's chest rises and falls. "You saved a naked picture of your classmate on your phone, correct?"

"Yes, sir."

"Then under the law, you're guilty. Do you understand what it means to have to register as a sex offender?"

"Yes, sir."

"That's what could happen if you get convicted. You don't want to risk that. Everybody says you're a smart kid. You're not thinking too smart right now."

"It's not right to put me in jail just for saving that picture," Graylin says. "And I'm going to prove it to the jury."

"How are you going to do that?"

"I'm going to convince them that I'm innocent when I testify."

The judge glares up at me, then back down at Graylin. "Your attorneys are putting you on the witness stand?"

"I have the right to testify in my own defense," Graylin says. "It's the law."

"Jesus Christ!" the judge exclaims. He points a lean finger inches from Graylin's nose. "This is what you're going to do, young man. You're going to take the next thirty minutes to discuss this with your attorneys. Then, you're going to listen to your father and your attorneys and—"

Graylin politely interrupts the judge. "I'm sorry, Your Honor, but I don't need any time. I'm not going to change my mind."

He reaches into the inside pocket of his jacket and pulls out some papers. I can see that it's a wrinkled copy of the pamphlet Jenny gave him the day after his arrest. It looks so worn he must've read it a dozen times.

"This is some information that my attorney gave me about my rights," Graylin says. His hands are shaking so badly we can hear the paper rattle. "And it says right here on page six that I get to make the decisions about my case."

In a shaky voice, he starts reading from the pamphlet.

*You are not required to accept a settlement offer. The decision to accept or reject the offer is only your decision. The defense attorney cannot make the decision for you, your parent or*

*guardian cannot make the decision for you, and the court*
*cannot force you to take a settlement.*

Graylin refolds the pamphlet and looks back up at the judge. His hands are no longer shaking.

The judge huffs loud enough to blow the curtains down. "Young man, I have the power to dismiss this case and send you back to juvenile court. Are you saying you don't want that either?"

"That's right, sir. I want my day in court."

Gus curses under his breath.

Graylin meets the judge's stern glare with more defiance than ever. "My granny always tells me to have faith," he says, putting the pamphlet back inside his jacket pocket. "So that's what I'm going to do. I'm not pleading guilty because I'm not a child pornographer."

# Chapter 54

### Angela

Once Graylin's little speech is said and done, one thing is clear, Judge Lipscomb is pissed. Pissed at the prosecution for not dropping the case, pissed at the defense attorneys for not being able to talk some sense into our client and pissed at Graylin for being too young and too naïve to understand the incredible risk he's taking with his life. But to our surprise, he doesn't send the case back to juvenile court.

The judge denies my request for a continuance but gives us the rest of the day off. He sends the jury home with instructions to return the following morning.

Jenny and I agree that we have to roll the dice and let Graylin testify. The jurors now know Kennedy set him up. If they're going to let him walk on the possession charge, they need to see for themselves, not through the testimony of others, what a great kid he is.

I take Graylin to Jenny's office where we spend the rest of the day going through mock questioning. Although only one charge remains, the stakes are still high. Except for a murder trial, I've never had a case with more serious consequences. Nor have I ever had a case where I wanted to win for my client more than this one.

After Gus drops by to pick up Graylin, Jenny and I sit in silence for a while.

"This is positively my last juvenile case," I say. "It's way too heart-wrenching."

Jenny smiles. "It is tough sometimes, but when I fight for these kids and win, there's no better feeling in the world." She stands up and pulls a large album from the top of a file cabinet. "This," she says, "makes it all worthwhile."

I open the album and find dozens of cards and letters, some handwritten, some typed. There are also a few pictures.

I look up at her. "Are these letters and cards from your former clients?"

"Yep."

I read a couple of them.

*Dear Ms. J.,*
*Thank you for beleeving in me. Nobody ever beleeved in me like you did.*

*Dear Miss Jenny,*
*Thanks for fighting for me. I promise I'm going to get my GED and stay out of trouble.*

There's a picture of Jenny posing with a gangly black kid in a cap and gown. "Who's he?"

"My star client," Jenny beams. "He graduated from El Camino Junior College last year. He'll be a junior at Long Beach State in the fall."

Reading the letters makes me feel hopeful and scared at the same time. I pray we'll see Graylin graduate from college one day.

"It'll be a good thing for the jury to hear from Graylin," Jenny says. "He's smart, kind and articulate. They'll see their own kids in him. They won't want to ruin his life."

I don't know how long I've been staring out of the window.

"Hey, are you even listening to me?" Jenny says.

I spin around. "I have an idea. Where's our witness list?" I frantically search for our trial binder.

"Why?"

"*Please* tell me we kept Dr. Mandell on the list."

Dr. Mandell is a child psychologist. We'd gone back and forth about whether we wanted to call an expert to testify.

"She's on there," Jenny says. "Why?"

I start scrolling through my phone for her number. "Because Dr. Mandell is going to help us get jury nullification."

"What do you need me to do?" Jenny asks.

"Pray that she's available on short notice."

# CHAPTER 55

## *Angela*

The next day, we complete the testimony of Graylin's minister, then call Dr. Faye Mandell to the stand.

The woman exudes professionalism. She's around sixty, slim and stylishly dressed in a hot pink pantsuit. After explaining that she specializes in child psychology, Dr. Mandell tells the jury that she has a master's degree in clinical social work and a Ph.D. in child psychology, both from USC. She's also written numerous books and articles on parenting and has appeared on CNN and MSNBC to discuss sexting among teens.

"Dr. Mandell, you've written several articles about the impact of technology on adolescent sexuality. Can you tell us how the two intersect?"

"Technology allows kids to explore their sexuality without doing it face-to-face. In my day, we talked in person or on the telephone. Today's teens don't talk, they text and sext."

"Can you explain to the jury what sexting is?"

"It's sending or posting sexually suggestive text messages and images, including nude or semi-nude photos—usually of yourself—via cell phone, email or social media."

"Is sexting a popular trend among teens?"

"Sadly, yes. A study published in the *Archives of Pediatric & Adolescent Medicine* found that thirty-nine percent of teens admit to having sent a sext. Another forty-eight percent say they've received one. A whopping eighty-six percent of teen sexters never get caught. And more girls sext than boys."

"And when you say teens, what ages are you referring to?"

"For the figures I just quoted you, thirteen to seventeen."

I hit a few buttons on my laptop, introducing an exhibit. An image of the brain appears on the courtroom screen.

"I'd like to ask you a few questions about childhood brain development. Is the brain of a teen, say a fourteen-year-old, the same as the brain of an adult?"

"No, it's not. The front part of the brain is called the prefrontal cortex. This area right here." She aims at the screen with a laser pointer. "It's responsible for problem solving, impulse control and weighing options. In children, this area isn't fully developed until the early to mid-twenties."

"What do you mean when you say a child's brain isn't fully developed?"

"As children enter adolescence around the age of twelve, a number of changes begin taking place. They start to develop sexually, which we call puberty. They also start developing their own identity and move away from their parents and closer to their peers. During this phase, kids are more apt to experiment. Today's technology makes it easier for them to take risks based on hyper-rational thinking, which is—"

"Objection, Your Honor," Sullivan interrupts. "We're not here for a biology lesson. I don't think this is at all relevant. And it's far more prejudicial than it is probative."

"Counsel, please approach."

"Ms. Evans, I tend to agree with the prosecutor. How is this relevant to the possession charge?"

"Your Honor, this is a specific intent crime. The prosecution has to prove that my client had the intent to possess child pornography. His maturity level and the development of his brain in that regard are directly relevant."

"I agree with you, Ms. Evans. Overruled," he says loudly.

I'm stunned. I expected Judge Lipscomb to give me more of a fight. I smile inwardly. He's still pissed that the prosecution didn't drop all of the charges and he's cutting us some slack.

I turn back to Dr. Mandell. "You were about to explain what hyper-rational thinking is. Please continue."

"Children generally lack the ability to correlate potential cause and effect. This makes them more vulnerable to things like peer pressure, drugs, and sexting. Because of the undeveloped nature of the prefrontal cortex, teens are also more likely to take risks that an adult would never take. Like sending a naked selfie or saving one they may have received from a text or Snapchat."

Sullivan audibly groans.

"So are you saying their maturity level impacts their behavior?"

"Absolutely. They aren't physiologically developed enough to understand the long-term consequences of their decisions. They're children. There's a reason we don't let fourteen-year-olds drink, drive, vote or smoke."

"Do you believe children should be charged with possession of child pornography for—"

"Objection!" Sullivan yells.

"Sustained," Judge Lipscomb replies, giving me a look that says I'm pushing the envelope. "Let's move this along, counselor."

"Dr. Mandell, why do you think sexting is so prevalent among teens these days?"

"In great part because our children are saturated with sexual images. TV, movies, music, advertising, everywhere they turn.

If you have the exhibit I prepared, I can show you better than I can tell you."

I hit a key on my laptop and a collage of photographs fills the courtroom screen.

"This is a sampling of the kind of sexual images our children are bombarded with almost from the cradle." She points the laser at the screen. "This is an ad for mascara that I saw in Macy's. It touts the mascara as *Better Than Sex*. And we've all seen the Carl's Jr. hamburger commercials where the ketchup runs down the woman's breasts. These are shots from *The Bachelor* and *The Bachelorette* TV shows, which are extremely popular among teenage girls. They show people making out within minutes of meeting each other."

She aims the laser at a picture of the *Housewives of Atlanta*.

"This is another popular reality show. As you can see, the women routinely dress in an extremely provocative manner, exposing their breasts. These shows set the standards for our kids. Then there's *Dating Naked*. I still can't believe that's even on TV. And, of course, there's the ever-popular Kim Kardashian, whose initial claim to fame was a porn video. Even in cartoons like *Shrek*, there's sexual innuendo."

Dr. Mandell places the laser pointer along the edge of the witness box.

"We can't bombard our children with sexual images and then expect them to act like saints. What you see up there on that screen is the norm for today's kids. So, of course, they don't think it's any big deal to trade pictures of their genitals."

I see several members of the jury—both male and female— frowning, but at the same time, nodding in agreement.

After a few more questions, I hand my witness over to Sullivan.

"Ms. Mandell, do you believe that teens should be absolved of their crimes simply because their brains aren't fully developed?"

Dr. Mandell smiles. "I'm sorry, Ms. Sullivan, but it's *Dr.* Mandell. And no, I don't think that. But I do think that—"

"That's okay. You've answered my question."

I stand up. "Your Honor, Dr. Mandell should be allowed to finish her response."

The judge peers down at the witness box. "Were you finished, Dr. Mandell?"

"No, I wasn't."

"You can continue."

"I just wanted to point out that the law hasn't caught up with technology. We're talking about sexually curious children, not pedophiles. We're criminalizing normative adolescent behavior."

Sullivan pounces. "So you believe a kid who keeps sexual images on his phone is engaging in normal adolescent behavior?"

"I sure do. Over seventy percent of teens own a cell phone. You'd be surprised at how many kids are sexting." She turns away from Sullivan and faces the jury. "Maybe even your own kids. As far as I'm concerned, any parent who hasn't had a stern talk with their teenagers about sexting is guilty of parental malpractice."

At least three of the female jurors have distressed looks on their faces. They're probably going to run straight home and check their kids' cell phones.

Sullivan seems uncertain about where to go next, but plows on.

"It sounds as if you think the only way we can keep kids from sexting is to confiscate their phones?"

"That's one way," Dr. Mandell says. "But until kids truly understand the consequences of doing this, it's ridiculous to lock them up and make them register as sex offenders for the rest of their lives."

A couple of jurors grimace. They didn't know finding Graylin guilty means he'll be branded an eternal sex offender. I could kiss Dr. Mandell for sneaking in that little jewel.

Sullivan asks a couple more questions that go just as badly, then gives up.

The judge dismisses Dr. Mandell then turns to me. "Who's your next witness, counsel?"

I'm holding my breath as I slowly rise. "Your Honor, I'd like to call Graylin Alexander to the witness stand."

# CHAPTER 56

## *Angela*

The judge gives us a fifteen-minute break. He must've seen the trepidation in my eyes and figured I needed it.

Jenny follows me to the ladies' room where I press cold paper towels to my face.

"I wish Mama Baker was here to lay hands on us," Jenny says.

I laugh. "Maybe we should give her a call to see if she can do it over the phone."

We're making jokes, but we both know this is no joking matter.

"I'm glad we teamed up on this case," Jenny says.

"Me too." I give her a long hug.

Jenny opens the bathroom door and steps aside to let me walk out first. "Let's go finish kicking Sullivan's butt."

Graylin, Gus, and Dre are standing outside the courtroom. I was so nervous about Graylin testifying today that I didn't notice his new suit.

"You're looking really good in that suit," I tell him.

He smiles. "My aunt Macie bought it for me."

"You ready to testify?"

"Yep."

"Now remember—"

"You don't have to tell me again, Ms. Angela. I remember. Only answer the questions asked. Say *yes, ma'am*, not *yeah*. Sit up straight. Be respectful. Don't show my feelings. Look the jurors in the eye. Did I miss anything?"

I chuckle. "No, I think you got it all."

Five minutes later, when it's time for him to take the stand, Graylin's confidence has shriveled up like a grape on a hot griddle. His knees are bouncing up and down and he's wringing his hands.

"Can you state your name for the record?" I begin.

"Graylin Michael Alexander."

"I'd like you to take a look at the document on the screen and tell us what it is."

His face shines with pride. "That's my last report card."

"And what is your grade point average?"

"Three-point-eight. I got mostly A's."

"Are you in the TAG Program?"

"Yes."

"Tell us what TAG stands for."

"The Talented and Gifted Program."

"And how long have you been in TAG?

"Always."

"Always?"

"Yes, since elementary school."

"Do you like school?"

"Yes. I'm going to be a lawyer when I grow up."

He must have come up with that overnight. When we prepped him, he told us he wanted to be a video gamer.

"Did you receive a picture via Snapchat on May tenth?"

"Yes."

"What did you do with it?"

"I took a screenshot of it."

"Why?"

"Because I was shocked to see it."

"Were you aware that having it on your phone meant you were guilty of being in possession of child pornography?"

"No, ma'am, I didn't know that."

"What did you intend to do with the picture?"

Graylin lowers his chin. "I was going to show it to my friend Crayvon, but that's it. But I didn't though."

"Were you going to put it on the Internet?"

"No, ma'am."

"Did you put it on the Internet?"

"No, ma'am. I wouldn't do that."

I ask him several more questions, not because I need to, but because I don't want to place him in Sullivan's clutches. But ultimately, I have to.

Once I sit down, Graylin closes his eyes and his lips start moving. It looks as if he's praying.

"Good morning, Graylin," Sullivan says. "I only have a few questions for you."

"Okay." Graylin rubs his palms together.

"Have you ever received any other inappropriate pictures on your cell phone besides the picture of Kennedy Carlyle?"

I nearly fall over jumping to my feet.

"Objection, irrelevant, vague and ambiguous as to *inappropriate*," I say. "And the probative value is outweighed by its prejudicial effect."

"Sustained," Lipscomb says, "but only because the question is a little vague. Ms. Sullivan, could you be a little more precise?"

Sullivan happily rephrases her question. "Have you ever received a naked picture of anyone else besides Kennedy Carlyle on your cell phone before?"

We asked Graylin that question and he said no. The fact that Sullivan is asking it means she knows something we don't. From the terrorized look on Graylin's face, he's either going to answer in the affirmative or lie.

"Um, yes, ma'am."

*How did Sullivan know this? Is this information she got from Crayvon?*

"How many times?"

"Two times?"

Graylin looks sheepishly at me. I'm trying not to look angry, so I don't make him more nervous than he already is. But I want to strangle him for not telling us this.

"Who was in the pictures?"

"It was just two grown white ladies. I didn't know the ladies."

"When did you receive them?"

"I'm not sure. Last year some time."

"Who sent you the pictures?"

"I don't know. Somebody on Snapchat."

"Did you save those two pictures to your phone?"

Graylin sits up straighter, like he's proud to answer this question. "No, ma'am."

Sullivan hesitates as if she isn't sure she wants to ask the next question. "Why not?"

Graylin hunches his shoulders. "I don't know. I didn't know the ladies. And I also didn't know Snapchat that good back then."

"So if you'd known how to use Snapchat better, would you have saved those pictures too?"

"I don't know. Maybe."

"And why did you save Kennedy's picture?"

Graylin's chest starts to heave like he's entering the early stage of an asthma attack. He takes a long time to answer. Sullivan waits.

"Ma'am, I don't know, but I didn't mean any harm. I didn't know Kennedy's picture was child pornography. I wasn't—"

Sullivan dives in to cut him off. "I have no further questions of this witness."

"I wasn't trying to hurt anyone." Graylin turns to face the jury as tears trail down his cheeks. "I'm not a bad person—"

"Objection!" Sullivan screams, but her protest goes unheeded by both Graylin and the judge.

I can't believe it, but Judge Lipscomb is staring down at Graylin with watery, empathetic eyes. He's actually biting his bottom lip. He doesn't say one word and lets Graylin continue his emotional plea to the jury.

"I'm a good student," Graylin sobs. "And I go to church every Sunday. Please don't make me a child pornographer!"

By the time Graylin gathers himself and walks back to the defense table, I'm thrilled to see more than a few moist eyes in the jury box.

# CHAPTER 57

## Angela

I was hoping the judge would call a recess and let us do closing arguments in the morning, but Lipscomb wants this case over and done with as much as we do. So after lunch, Sullivan and I are set to make our final appeal to the jury.

The only reason I'm still on my feet is because I'm amped up on caffeine and adrenalin. When this trial is over, I can't wait to pull the covers over my head and sleep for a week.

Sullivan's wearing a maroon suit that looks like she slept in it. Her eyes are bloodshot and she didn't wash her hair this morning or put on any makeup. When she stands to address the jury, I can relate to her weariness.

"Good afternoon, ladies and gentlemen," Sullivan begins. "There is only one count before you, possession of child pornography. The defendant testified that he saved a naked picture of Kennedy Carlyle to his phone. That is a fact. The defendant, therefore, is guilty.

"Please don't let the defendant's tearful plea prevent you from fulfilling your duty as a juror. You must put your personal feelings aside and render a decision based on the facts and the law. I respectfully request that you find the defendant guilty of possession of child pornography."

I'm not surprised that Sullivan didn't try harder. I don't have that option. I have to step up to the plate and swing for a homerun.

I stand up, woozy from skipping breakfast and lunch. I paste a smile on my face and approach the jury box.

"When I first spoke to you about this case," I begin, "I told you it was about a kid simply being a kid. Graylin Alexander saved a naked picture to his cell phone. He didn't take the picture. He didn't send it to anyone else. He simply saved it to his phone.

"You heard LaShay Baker testify that when she and Kennedy Carlyle set up this scheme to entrap Graylin, they knew he would save the picture to his phone because—in her words—everybody does. My client is not a pedophile or a sex offender.

I walk over and stand behind Graylin's chair. His hands are folded and resting on the table and he's sitting as straight as a toy soldier.

"To the contrary, this cherub-faced, fourteen-year-old is a rather extraordinary young man. He's managed to make almost straight A's despite being raised by a single father and having a drug-addicted mother whose whereabouts he doesn't even know. Although the state is prosecuting my client under a statute designed to punish pedophiles, Graylin Alexander is not a pedophile. It's up to you to rectify this travesty. We can't raise our children in a super-sexualized society with erotic images everywhere they turn and not expect them to be impacted. The adults of this world are to blame for this sexting phenomena. Not our children.

"I respectfully request that you return a verdict of not guilty. Please don't punish this kid for simply being a kid."

As I sit down, a tidal wave of exhaustion consumes me.

"You did really, really good, Ms. Angela!" Graylin says, full of enthusiasm. "We won. I know it!"

I'm not so sure, but I don't have the heart to dash his hopes. I keep quiet and return his hug. He leaves with Gus and Dre to pick up a snack, while Jenny and I remain at the defense table, too spent to move.

Sullivan walks over to us. "Nice job, counselors. You really fought hard for your client."

I don't want her olive branch. "We wouldn't have to fight so hard if the D.A.'s Office would exercise some discretion and stop filing pornography charges against kids who don't deserve it."

She shrugs and walks away.

Jenny and I are stepping into the hallway, when the judge's clerk calls my name.

"The judge wants both sides back in court," she says.

I glance at my phone. The jury hasn't even been out twenty minutes. "They can't be done deliberating already," I say to Jenny.

"Yes, they can." She's beaming like a *not guilty* verdict has already been rendered. "And a quick verdict in a case like this usually means good news for the defense. I'll go find Graylin."

# CHAPTER 58

## *Angela*

When Judge Lipscomb walks out of his chambers, he's not wearing his robe. His expression is so stern it scares me. "The bailiff has informed me that the jury has a question."

I'm stunned. Questions mean confusion and confusion isn't good.

"What's the matter, Ms. Angela?" Graylin asks. "Why do they have a question?"

Before I can answer, the bailiff comes out of the jury room and hands Judge Lipscomb a piece of paper. He reads it, then briefly closes his eyes.

"The jury wants to know if Graylin would serve time in an adult prison or a juvenile facility if he's convicted."

The judge's words feel like a punch in the stomach.

"I'm going to call them back in and tell them their question is inappropriate since their focus should be on the verdict, not the sentence, which is my job. Everybody should stay close. I suspect we could have a verdict very shortly."

I feel something shaking and realize it's Graylin's bouncing knee. He starts to quietly sob. I'm doing everything in my power not to join him. I place my arm around his shoulders and gently rock him.

Jenny reaches across Graylin and grabs my free hand. "I've had a couple of cases where the jury asked the craziest questions, but still found my client not guilty," she says. "And even if they do find him guilty, there's always the possibility that Judge Lipscomb could throw out the verdict."

I wish Jenny would just shut up. I don't want her getting Graylin's hopes up. Mine either. I failed him and now I have to deal with that. After a few more minutes, I hand a sobbing Graylin off to Jenny and walk to the back of the courtroom and fall into Dre's arms.

Another hour passes before we learn that the jury has reached a verdict. This time I'm sitting between Jenny and Graylin, instead of having him in the middle. Jenny probably thinks I want to be the one to console Graylin. I want the center spot so the two of them can console me. If Graylin is convicted, I'm going to be the biggest basket case in this courtroom.

The jury files back in. Nobody's looking at us.

The judge goes through all the perfunctory language, then asks the jury foreman to stand.

As it turns out, Juror No. 5 is the foreman. He has several family members in law enforcement. This is not a good sign. The foreman typically wields the most influence over other jurors.

I'm holding Graylin's hand to my right and Jenny's to my left.

"Have you reached a verdict?" Judge Lipscomb asks.

"Yes, we have," the jury foreman says sternly.

We watch as the verdict form is passed to the judge for an advance look, then back to the foreman, who begins to read. "We find the defendant Graylin Alexander not guilty of—"

I hear Gus cheer from the back of the room. A jubilant Graylin jumps to his feet and turns around to face his father. "I told you, Dad! I told you!"

Judge Lipscomb bangs his gavel. "Let's quiet down. Back in your seat, young man!"

I don't hear anything else because my own sobs drown out the foreman's voice. Graylin and Jenny are hugging me, but all I can do is press my forehead to the table and cry.

# EPILOGUE

## *Angela*

"Who's the man?" Graylin grins as he extends his arm for a fist bump with his dad.

"You're the man," Gus says, pulling his son into his arms.

The backyard of Graylin's aunt Macie's home is packed with friends and family. In the week since the trial ended, Graylin returned to school and is back to his old self. As it turns out, there was only one juror who was on the fence, but he finally came around. It was his question about where Graylin would serve his time that had us thinking they were coming back with a guilty verdict.

Kennedy and LaShay were offered deferred entry of judgment deals, which they both accepted, and were expelled from Marcus Prep. I also filed a defamation and emotional distress lawsuit against LaShay and Kennedy on behalf of Graylin. Suing a kid means you're suing their parents. The Carlyles' attorney has already requested a meeting to discuss settlement. Graylin's going to have a hefty college fund when it's all said and done.

I walk over to Jenny, who's standing over the dessert table with a piece of cake in one hand and an apple martini in the other.

"You're the greediest white girl I've ever met," I tell her.

She takes a sip of her drink. "I thought Mama Baker's cake was amazing, but this red velvet is to die for." She takes a bite. "Do all black people make amazing cakes?"

"Excuse me, but I think that's a racist question."

She hugs me. "Naw, we're homegirls now."

"No more drinks for you," I say. "And I'm also driving you home."

Graylin runs up to Jenny.

"Like I was telling you," he says, "I'm going to be an attorney one day, so I want to get started early. I'm good at researching stuff online. Until I finish law school and pass the bar, can you hire me as your paralegal, Ms. Jenny?"

"Wait a minute," I say. "What am I, chopped liver? How come you don't want to work for me?"

" I want to help kids and Ms. Jenny only represents kids. I'm going to be a juvenile defense attorney."

I give him a hug. "I think that's the perfect career for you."

He turns back to Jenny. "So are you going to hire me?"

"How are you going to get to work?" Jenny says. "You're not even old enough to drive yet. And what about your schoolwork?"

"I can work from home and we can have meetings on FaceTime or Facebook Messenger. And besides research, I can also take a look at your cases from a kid's perspective and give you my opinion. I can be your paralegal-slash-consultant."

"You know what? I think you've talked yourself into a job."

"Excellent. So when do I start?"

"Hold your horses. Let me take a look at my caseload and see if I have anything I need your help with."

"Okay. And I want twelve dollars an hour."

"Excuse me, but that's higher than the minimum wage."

"You can't get a paralegal *and* a consultant for minimum wage. And don't worry, you'll get your money's worth."

"Young man," Jenny says, amused, "you're going to make a great attorney one day."

"I'm starting out as an attorney," Graylin says with a grin, "but I plan on running things. So I'm going to be a judge."

# DISCUSSION QUESTIONS
## FOR *#ABUSE OF DISCRETION*

1. Do you think it was right for the two police officers to keep questioning Graylin after he told them he couldn't talk to the police without his father's permission?
2. Do you agree with the law that says lawyers must follow the instructions of their child client and not the parent?
3. Before reading *#Abuse of Discretion,* did you know that teens who sext could face child pornography charges?
4. Do you know anyone who has sent or received a sext?"
5. Why do you think teens engage in sexting?
6. Do you think children who sext should be charged with a crime?
7. What can be done to stop teens from sexting?
8. What is the earliest age a child should be allowed to have a cell phone?
9. What can parents and teachers do to help children understand that sexting can result in serious legal consequences?
10. Do you think parents should put monitoring devices on their children's phone so they can track what they do on social media?
11. Have you talked with your parents about sexting and online safety?
12. Google "teen sexting cases" and find five cases to discuss with your friends and parents.

# ACKNOWLEDGEMENTS

While I am a lawyer, I've never practiced juvenile criminal law. Therefore, in writing this book I turned to a number of attorneys who are on the front lines in the battle to protect the legal rights of children.

A big thanks to Shirley A. Henderson, Law Office of Shirley A. Henderson, a smart, caring Los Angeles attorney who answered my many, many questions about the juvenile criminal justice system. Thanks also for being such a diehard fan of my work and a dedicated defender of our children.

The teen sexting epidemic was first brought to my attention by my UC Berkeley Law School classmate Colin Bowen, a former criminal defense attorney who's defended many children facing sexting charges. Thanks for sharing your expertise.

Thanks to Sherri L. Cunningham, a dependency lawyer and Supervising Attorney with the Law Offices of Rachel Ewing, who was always willing to review my manuscripts on very short notice and help me understand the inner workings of the juvenile justice system.

Thanks also go to Faye Mandell, a psychotherapist and licensed clinical social worker who helped me in the area of early childhood development, Jeffery Probasco, former Director of Eastlake Juvenile Hall (thanks for the tour), Lori Lee Gray, L.A. County Deputy District Attorney (who's nothing like my imaginary prosecutors), and the Honorable Catherine Pratt, Commissioner, Compton Juvenile Court, a judge who's always looking out for our kids. Thanks for all you do.

# ABOUT THE AUTHOR

Pamela Samuels Young is an attorney and award-winning author of multiple legal thrillers. A passionate advocate for sexually exploited children, Pamela speaks frequently on the topics of child sex trafficking, sexting, online safety, fiction writing and pursing your passion. Pamela is also a natural hair enthusiast and the author of *Kinky Coily: A Natural Hair Resource Guide*. The former journalist and Compton native is a graduate of USC, Northwestern University and UC Berkeley's School of Law. She resides in the Los Angeles area.

To schedule Pamela for a speaking engagement or book club meeting via speakerphone, Messenger, Zoom, Skype, FaceTime or in person, visit her website at www.pamelasamuelsyoung.com or email her at authorpamelasamuelsyoung@gmail.com.

Pamela loves to hear from readers! There are a number of ways to connect with her on social media:

Facebook: www.facebook.com/pamelasamuelsyoung
Twitter: www.twitter.com/authorPSY
LinkedIn: www.linkedin.com/in/authorpamelasamuelsyoung
Instagram: www.instagram.com/authorpsy
Pinterest: www.pinterest.com/kinkycoily
YouTube: www.youtube.com/kinkycoilypamela